FINDING FAMILY AT SEABREEZE FARM

JO BARTLETT

Boldwood

First published in Great Britain in 2021 by Boldwood Books Ltd.

Copyright © Jo Bartlett, 2022

Cover Design by Debbie Clement Design

Cover photography: Shutterstock

A CIP catalogue record for this book is available from the British Library.

Paperback ISBN 978-1-80162-025-3

Large Print ISBN 978-1-80162-024-6

Harback ISBN 978-1-80162-023-9

Ebook ISBN 978-1-80162-026-0

Kindle ISBN 978-1-80162-027-7

Audio CD ISBN 978-1-80162-019-2

MP3 CD ISBN 978-1-80162-018-5

Digital audio download ISBN 978-1-80162-021-5

Boldwood Books Ltd
23 Bowerdean Street
London SW6 3TN
www.boldwoodbooks.com

For Peter, the best grandfather-figure my children could ever have had and proof that blood isn't always thicker than water xx

PROLOGUE

There's a danger, when a child no longer believes in you-know-who, that the magic of Christmas can be lost, but it was never that way for Freya. As soon as she stopped writing letters to the big guy in the red coat, her dad made it his mission to inject a new kind of magic into every festive season their little family shared. There were trips to a Christmas tree farm, singing carols at the old people's home, and even the time when he accidentally set light to the outside Christmas tree, as he was releasing Chinese lanterns with their wishes for the following year written on the side. According to Freya's dad, whoever it was who said those things should be banned had been dead right. They still laughed about it years later and had photos of the poor tree, which looked more like something out of a horror movie than a Yuletide welcome at the door. It was the stuff that memories were made of, and the thought of him whacking the burning tree with a spade, as he tried to put out the flames – Basil Fawlty style – still made her smile.

On Freya's fifteenth Christmas, her dad had a new idea. He called it Undercover Santa and her instinctive reaction had been to roll her eyes.

'I'm not dressing up, so you can think again if you've got us matching outfits.' Freya crossed her arms. She wasn't as embarrassed by her parents as a lot of her friends, but she wasn't being seen anywhere dressed up in matching Santa suits.

'You don't have to dress up. It's not about what we're wearing, it's about what we're doing.' He grinned and put an arm around her mother, Colleen, who looked a bit disappointed by the fact they wouldn't be dressing up.

'And what exactly *are* we doing?' Freya narrowed her eyes. Singing at the old people's home had been a lot more fun than she'd expected, but there'd been no chance of bumping into any of her mates from school there. If her dad expected her to sing in public, then he was going to be very disappointed.

'I've bought twelve gift cards, that's four each. We're going to go into town and find people who look like they could do with a bit of a helping hand for Christmas. Once you've chosen someone you think could use the gift card, to take a bit of pressure off, or who just appreciates knowing that someone cares, then you can hand them out.'

'Don't you think some people could find that offensive, John?' Colleen wrinkled her nose, probably imagining how she'd feel if someone made her a similar offer.

'You don't have to say *why* you're giving them out.' He laughed. 'After all, we don't want Freya telling people it's because they're wearing supermarket brand trainers!'

'Don't worry, Dad, you're the only person who'd be seen

dead wearing those.' Freya stuck out her tongue. Her father would wear anything as long as it kept his feet dry but, at fourteen, having the right logo on the side of her trainers was still pretty near the top of her priority list.

'My point is, all you have to say is that you're sharing a bit of Christmas cheer and that you hope they enjoy whatever they spend the money on.'

'I could give them all to the homeless guy in the underpass, but not if the vouchers are for McDonalds. Did I tell you that Chrissie bought him a burger with the money from her Saturday job? But when she gave it to him, he said, "no thanks, I'm a vegetarian". She couldn't believe it.' Freya shook her head, still shocked at the idea that anyone could turn down a burger.

'Of course he's not going to eat a burger, it's against his principles.' John looked at her levelly for a moment and handed her four of the cards. 'You'll get it one day, when you realise there's more to life than fast food and trainers. Really thinking about others is what Christmas is all about. You've got to look at the gift card and decide what kind of person could make the best use of it. I definitely think you should give one to the young man in the underpass, but you need to spread the giving out. Each person can only get one of your cards.'

'He's got a dog.' Freya looked down at the cards. 'The guy in the underpass, I mean. So maybe he could use the gift card from the supermarket to stock up on dog food? He looks like he really loves his dog, and it just sits there watching him the whole time he's busking. I don't know if he gets much money, though, the guitar he uses looks like it's got one of the strings missing.'

'Now you're getting it.' Her dad nodded. 'Let's head into town then, shall we?'

Three hours later, all the gift cards were gone, but there was something else Freya still needed to do.

'Shall we grab a hot chocolate before we go home?' Her mum turned towards her, as they drew level with Topsie's Tearooms, and she nodded.

'There's just a last-minute present I need to get, I'll meet you in there.' Freya was already heading a bit further down the high street. Luckily, she found what she needed in the first shop she tried, which was empty compared to almost everywhere else they'd been that day.

'Did you find what you were looking for?' Her dad looked up as she joined them at the table, just after the server had set down three hot chocolates piled high with whipped cream and chocolate sprinkles.

'Yes, thank you.'

'So, are you going to tell us what it is then?' Her mother gestured to the small bag on the table, emblazoned with the Merlin's Music logo.

'Guitar strings.' Freya spooned whipped cream into her mouth, but that didn't stop her spotting the confused expressions on her parents' faces.

'You don't play the guitar.'

'I know, Mum, but Johnny does.'

'Who's Johnny?' Dropping two sugar cubes into his hot chocolate, her dad raised his eyebrows. 'It is finally that time when I'm going to have to accept boys coming to the door to take you out? I'm not sure I'm anywhere near ready. I think thirty's a good age to start dating.'

'Oh Dad, not that again! It's not a boyfriend, don't worry.

Johnny's the homeless guy who plays guitar in the underpass, the one with the dog.' Freya looked up at them. 'He was so happy when he got the gift card, but he definitely had at least one guitar string missing and I noticed how worn out the rest of them looked; like they might snap at any minute. So I used the last of my birthday money to get him a new set. Can we take them down to him before we go home?'

'Of course we can. Oh love, I'm so proud of you.' Moving across to Freya's side of the table, her dad wrapped his arms around her.

'All right, not here. Someone might see us.' She squirmed away from his embrace, secretly pleased that she'd done something to make him so happy and suddenly understanding exactly why he'd wanted to play Undercover Santa.

'See, you might think Dad has madcap ideas.' Her mum smiled. 'But I bet one day you'll be doing this with your own kids at Christmas.'

'Yeah, maybe.' Freya's response was grudging, but her mum was right. One day she wanted to tell her children all about the traditions their grandfather had started, and the memories they'd built as a result. It was the kind of legacy parents should hand down to their children, wasn't it? It proved they were a family and that nothing would ever change that... Or at least, that's what she'd thought.

1

_____

'This really is the end, isn't it?' Freya strained to see over the pile of boxes stacked up in front of her.

'The end of an era, maybe.' Dropping a kiss on her forehead, Ollie grinned. 'But the start of something even more exciting.'

'London... you know what Mum would have said, don't you? Make sure you always wear your handbag strapped across your body and don't make eye contact on the underground.' She laughed at the memory. It might have taken eighteen months, but she could do that now, and it felt good.

'That last part is probably sensible advice!' Ollie pulled on his jacket and looked in her direction. He was tall, with dark curly hair and the kindest eyes Freya had ever seen. Depending on the light and the colour of the clothes he was wearing, they could look brown or green. Whatever the colour, they were the thing she'd fallen for first. 'I know this is a big change, but there's so much to look forward to. And we'll be able to go and see bands, or stand-up comedy, whenever we fancy it. Instead of deciding it's easier to stay in with the remote and a pizza.'

'Have I been boring you, Mr King?' Freya couldn't help laughing again, as he grabbed hold of her around the waist.

'Not for a moment, *very nearly Mrs King*. It'll just be exciting to start married life in a new city, with new jobs, and a million opportunities to do whatever takes our fancy. Although I'm hoping that staying in, and making our own entertainment, will still come into it on a pretty regular basis.' He kissed her neck. 'But if I start thinking along those lines, you are going to make me *very* late for work.'

'I can't believe we'll be married and in our new place in time for Christmas. When did we get so grown up?' As she pulled away from him, the unspoken answer was in his eyes – everything had changed with her mother's death. She wasn't sure if you could really be classed as an orphan at twenty-six, but she'd certainly felt like one.

'Give it another couple of years and we might be planning a family Christmas of our own.' Ollie touched the side of her face, another unspoken understanding passing between them. With only two blood relatives – one aunt, and a cousin who lived in Australia – Freya was desperate to fill the gap left by her parents' death. She wanted a big family. Five kids was the plan, although her auntie Linda had laughed and told her to see how she felt after the first one. But it was something she and Ollie had talked about before they'd got engaged, because she'd had to know he was up for being seriously outnumbered by their children. He'd seemed on board with all her dreams from the beginning, though, and she couldn't have got through the loss of her mother without him and his family. And somewhere along the line they'd become her family too.

One of the reasons for the move to London was to be closer to his parents, who'd relocated to Surrey, where his sister lived with her husband and two children. If there were going to be five more grandchildren in the mix, then grandparents living more locally was going to come in very handy, and maybe there'd be a move out to Surrey for Freya and Ollie at some point too. The thought of being surrounded by family like that made her smile, lifting the weight that had settled in her chest at the prospect of packing the last of their life in Bristol away. Her aunt's house just around the corner, and her parents' old place next door to that, were hard to leave behind. But Ollie was right, it was time to move on and leave some of the more painful memories behind them. No one could take the good memories away; they'd go with Freya wherever she went and whatever she did. She was the person she was because of her mum and dad, and holding on to some of their traditions was incredibly important to her as a result. That way she never really had to say goodbye.

'I'm going to see if I can find Mum's Christmas candy cane decorations, and make sure the box is left out, so we'll have them ready when we get to the flat. I know we won't be back until a few days before Christmas, but I still want to decorate the place.'

'I wish I could stay and help you, but there are a million loose ends to tie up before I can transfer to the London office.'

'Maybe we could meet for lunch?' Finishing work a month before the wedding to finalise all the plans for the big day, and the move to London, had seemed like a good idea at the time, but Freya missed the buzz of life on the ward more than she'd ever thought possible. Work had been her biggest distraction since her mother's death and she wasn't due to start her new job at a London teaching hospital until mid-January.

She was lucky to have so much free time, she knew she was, but it turned out that packing up a two-bedroom flat wasn't all that time-consuming, and the wedding seemed to more or less have organised itself after she'd put it in the hands of the team at Seabreeze Farm, where it was taking place. With all her friends at work, and Ollie doing twelve-hour days to get things straight before the transfer to his company's head office, Freya had far too much time to kill. And even more time to think.

'I'm sorry, angel, I'll be flat out today.'

'I know, I just thought you might be able to grab a sandwich, but maybe I can give Sophie a call and drive over to Bath to meet her?'

'She's gone to London for an interview. You know how desperate she is to follow us... well really *you* up there.' Ollie grinned. 'I could be offended that my oldest friend now prefers you to me, but let's face it, who wouldn't.'

'That's brilliant. I really hope she gets it; what's the job?'

'Head of HR at one of the American banks. I think it's more or less a done deal; her old boss works there and asked her to apply.' Ollie kissed her again. 'I'm sure she'll give you a call later, but why don't you give your auntie Linda a ring? It might be nice to have her here if you're going through your mum's stuff to find the decorations. Maybe you can look at some of the other boxes you took from your mum's loft too.

Then you can see what you want to take to the new place and whether there's anything Linda might want to keep.'

'Uh huh.' She couldn't bring herself to commit to doing that, even though she knew he was right. Going through the old photos and mementos her mother had filled several boxes with, and had stored in the loft of Freya's childhood home, would be like pouring salt into an open wound. 'Have a good day.'

'You too.' Ollie picked up his briefcase and kissed her one more time. It was just like hundreds of other mornings, so how could Freya have possibly known just how significant it would turn out to be.

* * *

'You shouldn't be waiting on me like this. You've got enough to do as it is, and I could hear you grunting from three rooms away when you were putting your boots on this morning.' Karen tried shifting position in the armchair but, with a plaster cast from thigh to ankle, even the smallest move was amazingly difficult. She didn't even want to think about itching it because as soon as she did, it would set off a chain reaction and there'd be an itch she couldn't get to, even with the aid of a knitting needle – a tool she'd resorted to out of desperation more than once.

'It's fine Mum, honestly. I'm pregnant not ill, and you need looking after for once.' Ellie moved to the back of the armchair and plumped up the cushions behind Karen's back, her baby bump filling the gap between them. Whatever her daughter said, this was hard on her, and Karen cursed herself for the hundredth time for being stupid enough to break both her tibia and her femur, chasing after one of Seabreeze Farm's rescued sheep – which had been nicknamed Holly Houdini for its ability to escape from almost any enclosure. It would have been fine if Karen's foot hadn't hit a rock and sent her sprawling forward. She might have saved herself by putting out a hand, and maybe ended up with just a broken wrist. Except she'd been gripping on to the lead rope with one hand, and her phone with the other, and the crack of her bones when the sound came had been unmistakeable. Holly had come trotting over to see what all the fuss was about, when Karen was lying on the ground wincing in pain. The silly sheep that had been the cause of all the trouble looked like butter wouldn't melt in her mouth and had stayed by Karen's side until Ellie came running down the hill, bump and all, and promptly burst into tears at the sight of her mother's leg at such an awkward angle.

'I feel like a complete burden, especially when Alan's out working and it all gets left to you. It would have to happen whilst our place is being renovated, too, so you're stuck with me the entire time! At least if I was there, you wouldn't feel like you had to check in on me every five minutes, as well as running the farm.'

'Do you seriously think I'd have left you over there, anyway?' Ellie grinned, suddenly looking like a little girl again, instead of a mother to be. Karen and Ellie shared the same blonde hair and hazel eyes, and Karen wondered briefly if the baby might inherit their colouring too. The thought of being a grandmother made her happier than she could ever explain and she couldn't wait. 'I love Alan to bits, Mum, but the idea of him being your nurse is pretty funny. You'd be sick to death of sausage and mash for a start.'

'He tries, though, bless him.' Karen had to smile too. Alan had come into both their lives when they'd inherited the farm from her Aunt Hilary almost four years before. He'd just been their curmudgeonly neighbour at first – Mr Crabtree – who seemed to resent their very presence. But things had changed when he'd realised they wanted to rescue the farm, instead of selling it off. Making an old donkey sanctuary into a viable business had proved more difficult than either of them would ever have believed, though.

The first step to turning it from a money pit, into something that could earn its keep, was getting permission to run it as a wedding venue. The farm's position on top of a cliff in Kent, which looked out across the sea and towards France on the horizon beyond it, had made it a popular choice from the beginning. There was a converted barn, a clifftop gazebo, and plenty of room for a marquee for bigger gatherings. But even that income wasn't enough to sustain them and their menagerie of animals during the winter months when there weren't many brides who wanted a wedding with a cold wind whipping straight off the sea.

The collection of animals left over from the donkey sanctuary, and the other rescue work Aunt Hilary had done over the years – which Ellie seemed determined to continue – cost significantly more to keep during the cold winter months. Not to mention the upkeep of buildings that had all seen better days by the time they'd moved in. At one time they'd feared they might even have to resort to selling the farm. Then a minor miracle, in the shape of a large agricultural insurance company, which had decided to host all its corporate events at the farm, had changed everything and their finances seemed to be on an even keel at last.

Moving to Seabreeze Farm had changed their lives in other ways too. Karen and Alan had gradually moved from friends to something deeper, and, after their wedding, Karen had moved to the house on Alan's farm which bordered the old donkey sanctuary. Ellie had married the local vet, Ben, and it was hard to imagine life before Seabreeze Farm these days. It was demanding, and Karen would normally be hard at work running the catering side of the business, but now everything was falling to Ellie, and the small team of staff who helped out. Her daughter could protest all she liked, but Karen was going to feel guilty until she was back on her feet.

'Oooh.' Ellie suddenly grabbed hold of her bump. 'This little chap is making his presence felt today.'

'Is he kicking?' Karen reached out to place a hand on Ellie's stomach. It was a close contest as to who was the most excited about the baby's imminent arrival – Karen and Alan as grandparents to be, or Ellie and Ben as mum and dad. The baby was due in the first half of January, but Karen couldn't help hoping that things might happen a tiny bit more quickly. After all, what better Christmas gift could anyone get than the arrival of their first grandchild?

'I think it's Braxton Hicks.' Ellie put her hand over Karen's and pressed it against the bump. 'And I guess we should stop saying *he* all the time, or we're all going to struggle if he turns out to be she.'

'Has Ben forgiven you yet for not finding out what you're having?' Karen looked up at her daughter. There was something even more exciting about not knowing what gender the baby would be, but she could understand her son-in-law's frustration. It was like the temptation to lift the corner of the wrapping on the biggest present under the tree, and take a quick peek inside, but Ellie had been adamant from the outset.

'He's okay with it now, especially since he's realised it means Daisy can't coerce us into a gender reveal!' Ben's sister was a nice enough girl, but she'd throw a party to celebrate the opening of a fridge door and she couldn't be more different from her brother.

'We'll find out soon enough and he, or she, is going to have so many cuddles from Nana, they're going to wish there were two of them to share the load!' Karen laughed at the look that crossed her daughter's face.

'Oh don't wish that on me, or it might happen next time around. I kept dreaming about twins before the first scan and I almost kissed the sonographer when she said there was only one in there. Although I think Ben was even more relieved than me.'

'I can understand why twins might have felt a bit over-whelming, especially given how busy you both are. How are things for Ben at the surgery? Any sign of David making it back to work?' Karen tried shifting again, but there didn't seem to be such a thing as a position that was comfortable for more than about ten minutes at a time.

'No, he's got a date for the surgery on his back now, but Ben is stuck with locum vets for the time being, probably well into the New Year. I just hope he's going to be able to take a bit of paternity leave.' Ellie pulled a face. 'I know I pushed the stable conversion through for the King/Halliwell wedding, but I'm beginning to wish we didn't have so much on. I've got cankles the size of tree trunks, where my calves and ankles have merged into one, and the only wedding toast I feel like making is with a large glass of Gaviscon.'

'Can you book some more casual staff? I know you keep saying you're not ill, but this just goes to show you need to take it a bit easier. The wedding's only a few weeks before your due date, isn't it? Most people in normal jobs have gone on maternity leave by then.'

'This isn't a normal job though, is it?' Ellie raised an eyebrow. 'The Kings have got The Old Stables for the week after the wedding, and we've only got one Christmas party and the fundraiser after that. So I can take it easy then.'

'Aside from looking after the animals, that is. Oh and getting everything ready for the baby's arrival.' Karen hadn't missed the fact that Ellie had rescued two more donkeys, who the RSPCA had wanted to re-home after finding them neglected in a field and no one had come forward to claim them. Ellie was a chip off Aunt Hilary's old block and telling her she had too much on her plate was a waste of breath. Karen would just have to have a word with Ben and Alan, to make sure they kept an eye on her.

'Liv and Seth finish at the school in the second week of December, for the holidays, and they've both said they'll come up to help with the Christmas events we've got booked in, and Alan's even agreed to stand in for Derek and be Santa at the fundraiser.' Ellie stuck out her belly. 'Although I think I could have given him a run for his money this year with this thing.' Liv was Ellie's childhood friend, who'd settled back in Kelsea Bay after coming home for Ellie and Ben's wedding. Liv worked at a local private school, with her partner, Seth, who was an old friend of Ben's. It was relief that

Ellie had other support close by and everyone was rallying around. Although it made Karen feel guiltier than ever that they were having to give up their free time too.

'There must be something I can do, instead of just sit here. Hopefully, they'll let me have the cast taken off and get a fracture boot by the time the fundraiser comes around, or at least get it down to half a cast. It'll have been ten weeks since the accident, by then, and my femur has got enough metal work in it to shore up the cliff face. So even supporting a body as chunky as mine shouldn't be too much of an issue!' Baking for a living meant that diets never lasted much beyond the time it took for the latest batch of cupcakes to rest on the cooling rack. But Alan never seemed to notice the bits that carried on wobbling for far longer than they should after they'd driven over the cattle grid that separated the two farms. And everyone wanted a cuddly grandma, didn't they?

'You just take it easy for now. Doing the emails and answering the phone helps more than you know, and it's one less thing for me to worry about.' Ellie planted a kiss on her mother's head. 'I'll be back in an hour or so, and we can stop for tea and a bit of cake if you like?'

'Who made the cake?' Karen held her breath. The last time Ellie had attempted a Victoria sponge, it had ended up with a bit more crunch than she'd intended, when a few bits of eggshell had slipped through. But mixing up the home-made jars of strawberry jam, with cranberry sauce, was what had really made it inedible.

'Don't worry, this one's all down to Mr Marks and Mr Spencer.' Ellie stopped when she got to the lounge door. 'But if you don't do as you're told and rest that leg, I will make all the desserts for Christmas this year.'

'That, my darling, would be a cruel and unusual punishment!' Karen blew her daughter a kiss, and held in a sigh. Checking the emails would have to be enough for now, and Ellie was right, they only had a few things to get through before Christmas. But like the half-hidden rock that had sent her hurtling into a crumpled heap on the ground, the unexpected was always just around the corner.

2
——————

Freya ran a hand through her long dark hair and looked down at the box in front of her. The words *'Memories and Family Photos'* were written across the cardboard in familiar big red letters. Her mother, Colleen, had always labelled everything thoroughly, and Freya had been the only one at secondary school who'd had a name tag in her socks as a result. Focusing on the writing, she wrestled with the urge to stick another label on the box, ready for the move, without even looking at the contents. She'd made two cups of coffee and sent several texts to delay opening it already. There were photos of her parents around the flat, of course, but looking back at pictures from when Freya was a baby had just been something she hadn't been able to face. They'd been young and in love, with a whole lifetime stretching in front of them, but they'd barely made it to fifteen years of marriage before her father had died, and her mother had never been quite the same after that. It was painful to stare all those lost hopes in the face, knowing that their life didn't turn out as they'd hoped. But there were bound to be happy memories in there too and, eighteen months on, the thought of looking back on high days and holidays seemed worth getting past the inevitable tears for. Taking a knife out of the kitchen drawer, Freya drew it down the centre of the parcel tape and pulled back the cardboard flaps, suddenly excited at the prospect of what she might find. Twenty minutes later, nothing would ever be the same again.

'Freya, it's you! I thought there was a fire the way you were hammering on the back door.' Auntie Linda stepped to one side just in time, otherwise she might have been knocked off her feet by Freya charging through the door that led from the back garden straight into the kitchen. 'What on earth's the matter, lovey?'

'He's not my dad is he?' Freya searched her aunt's face, as she waited for a response.

'What are you talking about?'

'John, of course! He not my real father, is he?'

'What on earth makes you say that?' Linda screwed up her face, but Freya didn't miss that there was no immediate denial, or the way her aunt's face and neck seemed to flush bright red. If she'd somehow got it wrong, then surely her aunt would have dismissed the idea straight away. Wouldn't she?

'I was going through some boxes Mum left in the loft, old photos and that sort of thing. But then I found a jewellery box, with a photo.'

'What photo?' Auntie Linda was still doing her best to maintain a neutral expression, except for the tiny twitch in her right eye and the fact she was still glowing like a Belisha beacon.

'Mum and a man. I'm guessing she would have been in her mid-twenties, so not long before she had me. She had her hair half over her face, but there used to be a photo of her in the hallway at home, where she had the exact same hairstyle, from around the same time. So I know it's her.'

'And?' Auntie Linda let out a long breath. 'I'm sure she had other boyfriends before John, in fact I know she did. But I still don't get how that's led you to the conclusion that he wasn't your dad?'

'There was a journal in the jewellery box too.' Freya had hardly got the words out before Auntie Linda's hand flew to her mouth. Even before she uttered a word, there was no doubt in Freya's mind now that she'd been right – her aunt had never been good at hiding what she was thinking and this time it was written all over her face.

'Did you read it?'

'Enough of it to know that she didn't meet John until I was two.' Freya's voice was shaking; it was still almost impossible to believe, despite the words literally spelling the truth out. 'I always believed the story that they didn't put Dad's name on my birth certificate because they'd split up few times before I was born, and Mum didn't want to do it unless they were married. When I asked why there were no photos of Dad holding me as a baby, I believed the lies about that too – that Mum couldn't take a photo without chopping everyone's heads off, until digital cameras were invented, so Dad had taken all the early photos. How many other lies did they tell me?'

'She used the journal to cope with everything that happened. I think writing it all down helped her to process it. I thought I'd got rid of everything before she died. I

promised her I had.' Linda's eyes filled with tears and she
was shaking her head. 'I let her down; you were never meant
to find out.'

'Well that's all right then. Although knowing that you
lied to me, too, doesn't help, funnily enough.' Freya slapped
the journal down on to the kitchen counter, wishing that
Auntie Linda had accomplished her mission and made sure
the family secret stayed safe. But opening that journal had
been life changing, and now there was no way back. 'Why
didn't she just burn the bloody thing years ago, if she didn't
want me to find out?'

'In the beginning her plan was to tell you as soon as you
were old enough to understand. She always kept a diary,
right from when she was a kid and I spent half my time,
when I was still living at home with her, trying to find out
where she'd hidden it, so I could read what she was up to.'
Linda gave a half-smile. 'But then John begged her not to tell
you. He didn't want to lose his little girl, if you found out
more about your birth father. I don't think she could bring
herself to throw the photos and the journal out, because
they meant a lot to her. But when she was ill, she asked me
to make sure there was nothing left up there. I found a few
photos and another journal from around the time she fell
pregnant, but I must have missed the jewellery box somehow. I promised her it would be okay, that you wouldn't have
to know, and I let you both down.'

'Why didn't she tell me when Dad died?' Freya wasn't
sure if she should even be calling him that any more, but
after so many years of using that label, it was impossible to
just use his name. She couldn't even process the thought
that the man she'd loved so much, and who'd shaped every-

thing about the way she lived her life, hadn't been who she thought he was.

'Your mum talked about it from time to time, but she thought it might upset you even more if you found out the truth. And when she got the diagnosis she didn't want to rake all that up.' Auntie Linda filled the kettle as she spoke, as if searching for something normal to do in the midst of a revelation that had left Freya feeling like even the kitchen tiles beneath her feet were shifting – like sand in a storm.

'Who was he? My *real* father.' Freya fixed her eyes on her aunt's face again, the words sounding alien as she said them out loud. Part of her still couldn't believe it was true. Her father had been the best man she'd ever known, until she'd met Ollie and had finally found someone who might match up to him. But now it felt like she hadn't really known him at all.

'Oh lovey, I'm really sorry, but I don't know.'

'Please don't lie to me.' Freya's tone sounded harsh even to her own ears, but she couldn't help it. Whatever promises Linda had made to her mum, they were null and void now the secret was out.

'I'm not lying, I promise.' Linda reached out, but Freya flinched. She'd discovered that the people she'd trusted most in the world had been lying to her in the worst possible way. She didn't want comfort, just the answers to some of the hundred or so questions already burning at the back of her brain. 'At least come through to the sitting room, so Mrs Rogers can't look over from her conservatory and try to lip read everything we're saying. I caught her watching me with binoculars last week, and I'll have to get your uncle Dave to add another couple of feet to the garden fence at this rate.'

'Oh, so there's *someone* else who isn't already in on the secret, then? I thought even Mrs Rogers might have found out before me.' Freya couldn't keep the bitterness out of her voice. Deep down she knew none of this was really Auntie Linda's fault, but without her parents around to confront, she was getting the brunt of the backlash. It might not be fair, but finding out at twenty-eight that your dad wasn't really your dad, was hardly fair either. It hurt like hell.

'Please, Freya, don't be like this.' The tears were spilling out onto Linda's cheeks now. 'Just go through to the lounge and let me bring the tea in, so I can at least try to explain properly. Please. I can't lose you too, it would kill me.'

Guilt prickled at Freya's scalp, and it was obvious how hard this was for Linda. She was putting her aunt in an impossible position, but she had to find out as much as she could, so she could try to make sense of it. And if she wasn't really a Halliwell, then who was she?

She walked through to the lounge, which looked like Santa's grotto. The all-out celebration of the upcoming festivities was a stark contrast to the nausea that had been swirling in her stomach since reading the words in her mother's journal, dated two months after Freya would have celebrated her second birthday.

June 15th, 1993

John asked me to marry him! He wants to take Freya on as his own and I know the three of us will be happy together. Mum always said the past was best left in the past and now I know what she meant.

The words had swum in front of Freya's eyes, as she'd

somehow landed on that very entry – in a journal that must have been two hundred pages thick. It was almost as if fate had intervened and someone, somewhere, had finally been ready for her to discover the truth. Not that she believed in all that, it was just dumb luck. Good or bad, she was yet to decide, but right now the only word she could use to describe it was devastating. As she looked at the sea of baubles twinkling on the tree across the room, it was like she was on autopilot. When she finally spoke again, even her voice sounded robotic. Nothing felt real.

'I see you haven't stinted on the decorations, even though you're away for Christmas.' Freya turned to face her aunt and forced a smile that made her cheeks hurt, guilt sweeping over her again at the lack of colour in the older woman's face. None of this was Auntie Linda's fault and she was all Freya had left of her mother. She couldn't afford to let the secret she'd kept sour their relationship, no matter how hard that might be when it was all still so raw.

'You know me, lovey. I never stint on the Christmas decorations and, as soon as my birthday's over on the twentieth of November, up they go. Scotty always said they were tacky and old-fashioned, but your uncle Dave never minds as long as I'm happy.' Linda shrugged. 'He might insist on keeping his old underpants until there are enough holes in them to strain spaghetti through, but I'm lucky to have him. And your mum was lucky to have John, you could see they were made for each other from the moment they met. Your nanna was over the moon to see both her girls settled, and we all thought John was right when he said there was no need to tell you that he wasn't your biological father. He loved you as much as any man could love their child.'

'I know.' There was a huge lump in her throat. She could picture her father saying those exact words and when she closed her eyes, she could almost hear him saying them. That's what made this all so hard, that and the fact that she'd never be able to talk it through with him.

'I understand this is a huge shock, but knowing your dad like you did and knowing how much he loved you, do you think any good can come from wondering what might have been?'

'I'm really not sure, but do you know what hurts the most?' Freya picked up the mug of tea Linda had pushed towards her. 'The fact Dad thought I'd reject him, or think less of him, just because he wasn't my biological father. Is that the sort of person he really thought I was? Because that must be why he didn't tell me.'

'Oh lovey, you were two years old when he made that decision; he didn't know how good your relationship would turn out to be, did he? Maybe it was because he saw how Scotty was with me and your uncle Dave at the time – I think he'd just turned thirteen when John married your mum and he'd regularly announce that he hated us both, even in front of company.' Linda laughed this time. 'But he grew out of it, and he'll even admit to missing me, now that he's almost forty and is living on the other side of the world!'

'Do you ever wish you'd had more kids? There's almost nothing left of this family, with Mum gone, and Scotty in Australia. I grew up longing for brothers and sisters, but I'd happily have traded that for a few more cousins, and I ended up with neither. I could never get Mum to give me a straight answer about why I'd never had any siblings, but she must have told you.' Freya reached out and squeezed Linda's hand. She had a feeling she knew the answer, but if they were going to open up the box of family secrets they might as well reach right down to the bottom.

'Is it me, or is getting cold in here?' Linda stood up and flicked the switch to turn on the imitation wood burner, which had an equally artificial plastic garland pinned in swags above it.

'Stop changing the subject.' Freya patted the empty seat beside her on the sofa. 'Just tell me what you know, please.'

'Well I can tell you why your uncle Dave and I didn't have any more kids after Scotty.' Linda sat down again, the glow from the artificial flames giving the room a slightly orange hue. 'That boy had reflux for the first two years of his life and didn't sleep in his own bed until he turned six! Your uncle Dave couldn't have got near me, even if I'd wanted him to.'

'Six years, really?' Freya had never been as close to Scotty as she'd liked to have been. An age gap of well over ten years had seemed huge when they were younger. And it was just starting to close when he'd emigrated with his wife, who was originally from Australia, when she found out she was expecting their first child. Freya knew how hard it had been for Linda to have her only child move so far away, even though she'd tried to hide it.

'Yes and when I could finally face thinking about going through all that again, I just sort of figured the time had passed. Scotty was at school, and we had our life back. After all, we had a bit of alone time to make up for!' Auntie Linda laughed and Freya tried hard not to pull a face.

'Now I know why you keep telling me to see what it's like having one baby, before I decide to have five.' Freya squeezed her hand again; Linda was the closest thing she had to a mother figure and she'd already forgiven her for keeping her parents' secret; she hadn't had a choice. 'But what about Mum and Dad? If Dad was willing to take on a ready-made family, why didn't he have one of his own?'

'As far as he was concerned, he did! You were every bit his daughter, and I know he never felt as though he'd missed out.'

'Do you think they didn't have more children because he was frightened he wouldn't love me as much as the others?'

'That's probably the silliest thing I've ever heard.' Linda put down her cup with a thud. 'They tried for years to have another baby, *because* they loved having you so much, but it just never happened. They didn't want to go down the route of finding out why and your dad told me more than once that it had been an easy decision to make, because they were so thankful they had you.'

'And what about my father... my biological father. Did mum even tell him I existed?'

'Before you ask me again, I promise you that I don't know who he is and I don't think trying to find out is going to do you any good.' Linda's expression was uncharacteristically stern. 'But she did tell me she wrote to him and never heard back. She tried to find him, just after you were born, to let him know he had a daughter – because she couldn't believe he wouldn't want to be part of your life. But he'd gone overseas and the letter she left with his family to pass on went unanswered. She didn't want to tell them about you before he knew, but she decided when he didn't make contact, after her final letter, that you were better off without him. Your nanna and granddad always spoilt your mum, probably because she was a fair bit younger than me, and they rallied round her once you were born. You were the apple of all their eyes and mine too. You were the little girl I never had. Your mum figured she didn't need your dad, and you didn't need him either, not when you had all of us. Then she met John, of course, and you know the rest.'

'I still can't believe she didn't tell you who my father was?'

'She didn't want to tell anyone else who your father was, until he knew. She thought it was only fair.'

'And when she went to tell him about me, where did she go? Maybe if I knew where he lived, I could find out more.' Freya was still in shock, but one thing was suddenly clear: she wanted to know more. With her mother gone, and half the secret with her, piecing together as much information as Auntie Linda could offer up was probably her only hope.

'Oh lovey don't do this, please. I can't bear the thought of you getting hurt. The only time I saw your mum cry about anything to do with you was when your biological father wasn't interested in getting in touch. But she wasn't crying for herself, she was crying for you. The thought of you being rejected again breaks my heart and that's if you manage find him.'

'I know there's a good chance I'll end up disappointed whether I track him down or not, but I can't just pretend he doesn't exist, and, if he is out there, I want to at least try.'

'She went to Kelsea Bay. She was working down there at a holiday park during the summer season when she fell pregnant with you, but that's all the information I have.'

'Kelsea Bay?' Freya felt the first piece of the puzzle click into place. It explained a lot. 'That's why she took me down there every summer? Do you think she hoped she might bump into him again?'

'I don't think so. She always loved it there, and she'd spent the previous two summers down there, before the year she fell pregnant with you.' Auntie Linda shook her head. 'I think she just wanted you to love the place as much as she did, so you'd have some connection with your father, even if you never knew who he was.'

'Well it worked, didn't it?' Freya had fallen in love with Kelsea Bay over the years, and the week she'd spent there with her mother every summer – just the two of them – had seemed all the more precious when she'd died. It was why she'd booked the wedding at Seabreeze Farm, which was perched on the clifftop just above Kelsea Bay. It had seemed like the closest thing to having her mother at the wedding.

'I wish I could tell you something else, but I could never get your mum to change her mind and tell me who he was. Not even at the end, and I'm so sorry you had to find out this way. I wish to God I'd done what I said I would and not put you through this at all.' There were tears welling up in Linda's eyes again and Freya didn't want to leave it like this.

'It's okay. I still can't get my head around it all, but I'm glad I know. At least I think I am.' Freya leant closer to her aunt. She was certain now that Linda was telling the truth about not knowing her father's name. It really was a secret her mother had planned to take to the grave.

'I'll talk to your uncle Dave, too, and see if he remembers anything else. Maybe your dad – John – opened up to him about something he's never mentioned to me.' She shrugged. 'It's worth a try, isn't it?'

'Thank you.'

'It's the least I can do after messing this all up so badly.'

'Whatever happens, I'm glad you did and I'm sorry I shouted at you earlier. I was just so shocked... and angry.'

'You had every right to shout.'

'No I didn't, not when you were just doing what Mum asked. I've got to try and understand that she and Dad did what they thought was best for me, and that they always did, otherwise I'm frightened it'll taint all the good memories I have of them. And that I won't be able to work out which of my memories are real and which are fantasies I've made up in my head. It all feels like it was a bit of dream right now.'

'You're in shock, but I promise you that every good memory you have of them is real. You were their world and they were both so proud of you.'

'I'll miss you this Christmas.' Freya swallowed hard.

'I'll miss you too, lovey. But this is such an exciting time for you and I hope that none of this spoils it. By Christmas you'll be married and starting your new life, and I'll be driving Scotty mad, nagging him to make his place a bit more festive, or turn it into a tinsel jungle as he puts it!'

'I can't believe you're flying out the day after the wedding.'

'I wouldn't have missed your big day for the world and Scotty was so sorry they couldn't make it, but with three kids under ten, and another on the way, I think a trip to the supermarket is a big adventure these days.'

'I can't wait to see him in the spring.' Freya smiled properly for the first time. It had been Ollie's idea to delay their honeymoon for a few months, so they could go out to New Zealand and then on to Australia to visit Scotty and his family. They were having a few days in the newly converted stable block at Seabreeze Farm, immediately after the wedding, but then it was straight on to the apartment in London and the start of a new life as Freya King. Except now it wasn't quite as simple as swapping the name Halliwell for King. There was another name, which was part of who she was, somewhere out there. Despite her aunt's concerns, she had to track that part of her history down and there was one person she knew who would do everything he could to help her.

* * *

The drive from Linda's house to Ollie's office in the centre of Bristol took less than twenty minutes, and for once Freya found a space in the first car park she tried. Bristol city centre might not have been a patch on her aunt's front room, in terms of Christmas bling, but the far more tasteful town-centre decorations were already up, and there were some lovely festive displays in several of the shop windows as Freya walked towards the block where Ollie's office was situated. There was one display, in the window of a gift shop, depicting a snowy village set on a hillside, which reminded Freya of Kelsea Bay. Not that there'd be any snow for the wedding – Kelsea Bay was about as far southeast as you could get, without actually falling into the sea, and it had the warmest climate of anywhere in the UK. It had made the week that Freya and her mother spent there every summer all the more magical as a result, because they could spend the day on the beach more often than not, searching for starfish and moon snail shells, especially those that had a hint of pink. It also meant that the prospect of snow was about as likely as Freya being able to find her father, without even knowing his name.

The receptionist in Ollie's building, Millie, waved Freya through as soon as she spotted her. They'd spent at least half an hour chatting about wedding plans at the company's summer barbecue, having discovered they were both having their ceremonies in December, and Freya made a mental note to ask Millie how things were going on the way out. She hadn't wanted to phone ahead and let Ollie know she was coming, or she'd have blurted out her discovery then and there. If she'd done that, he'd have been worried about how she was taking it and he might even have come home. He was under a lot of pressure as it was, getting home later and later the closer they got to the big move. He'd already said he hadn't got time for lunch, so losing half a day would have made the run up to the wedding even more stressful for him. She didn't need much of his time, but she had to see him face to face, even if it was just for five minutes. Freya needed him to tell her what she already knew, deep down – that she was still the same person she'd been when they'd kissed goodbye that morning. If she could make herself believe that nothing had really changed, she might stand a chance of not becoming completely obsessed by the desire to know who her father was. Anything was worth a try.

'Hi Jeremy. Sorry to just drop in like this, and I know Ollie's really busy today, but is there any chance I could just pop in and talk to him for five minutes?' Freya stood in front of his assistant's desk; nothing he said would persuade her to leave again without speaking to her fiancé first. Even if she had to wait two hours for him to come out of some boring board meeting, she was prepared to do it.

'Oh no, I hope you haven't come into town just to see him? I thought he'd have told you he's having a working lunch at Le Debut. He asked me to clear the diary as he won't be back for a couple of hours.'

'It must have slipped my mind.' Freya shook her head, trying to work out why Ollie hadn't told her the real reason he wasn't free for lunch. Maybe he was working on a deal he didn't want to talk about. He did that sometimes, when it was something he didn't want to jinx. 'Is he with a client?'

'I really don't know; it could be part of the handover to the new regional director who'll be taking over from him down here. I just update the diary when he tells me to.' It might have been Freya's imagination, but she could have sworn she saw two spots of colour appear on Jeremy's cheeks. 'Do you want me to give him a message?'

'No, it's fine. It's not important; I'll talk to him about it tonight.'

'So you're not going over to Le Debut to meet him then?' Jeremy looked as though he was counting on her saying 'No'. Maybe he thought he'd said too much already, but he had no way of knowing that Ollie going to their favourite restaurant for a business meeting – instead of meeting her for lunch – was the least of her worries. If it had been her job to enter-tain clients while talking about corporate data protection security, she'd have wanted a decent meal thrown into the mix, too, and probably a very large bottle of wine. But she didn't want Jeremy to give Ollie the heads up, either, and give him the chance to put her off. There was no way she could wait until tonight to talk to him and she'd happily wait however long she needed to at the restaurant, as long as she could speak to him.

'No, I'm going to head home, I've got loads of things to do before the wedding.' It was a lie, but only a tiny one in comparison to the secrets she'd unravelled that morning and she was beginning to wonder if there was anything left that she could believe in.

* * *

Ellie smoothed the bedspread down and stepped back to check there was nothing else that needed doing before Ben took the promotional photographs. Freya Halliwell and Ollie King would be the first guests at The Old Stables after their wedding, but Ellie was determined to add the option to book the accommodation to the website ready for the New Year. If it worked out, there were a few more outbuildings that offered scope for conversion, and Ellie had loved picking out the soft furnishings and dressing the rooms. The Old Stables had a large bedroom, with a king-size bed, an ensuite complete with a roll top bath, big enough for two, and a cosy open-plan kitchen/diner and living room.

'It looks good doesn't it?' Turning to her husband, Ellie smiled as he nodded. 'I could do with a week or two here myself.'

'I wish you *would* have a rest. We could get some extra help in for the farm, and someone to look after your mum.' Ben stood behind her and put his arms around where her waist used to be. If she got much bigger, his hands weren't going to be able to meet in the middle any more.

'Mum would hate that; she's frustrated enough as it is.' Ellie leant into him, stretching out the kinks in her back. 'I don't have to do that much for her anyway.'

'Maybe not, but on top of everything you already have to do, I'm worried it's too much. And I feel like the worst husband in the world, leaving all this to you most of the time.' He turned her around to look at him. 'I think we should up the number of casual staff working over Christmas at least.'

'Once we get the wedding out of the way, there's only the Agri-Rescue Christmas party and the fundraiser to get through before I can have a bit of a break.'

'You think having a baby is going to be restful?' Ben grinned.

'You'll be off for Christmas when you're not on call, won't you? So I was planning on leaving it all to you, whilst I hide out here.'

'It's a deal. You know I'd do anything for you, don't you?'

'Uh huh.' Ellie tilted her face up towards his. 'We're going to be all right at this parenting thing, aren't we?'

'Of course we are. You're not seriously worried about it, are you?'

'I forgot to feed Ginger this morning.' Ellie sniffed; she was determined not to cry again over something so stupid, especially when she'd given the little terrier a more than double-sized dinner to make up for it. 'How am I supposed to look after a baby when I can't even look after a dog?'

'It'll be fine. We all forget stuff and there's loads going on at the moment.' Ben pulled her back towards him. 'I wasn't going to tell you this, but the real reason I changed my phone was because I left the other one in the barn at Julian's, and one of the goats tried to eat it. I drove back to the farm like a bat out of hell, when I realised where I'd left it, but it was already beyond repair and drowning in goat saliva by the time I got there.'

'So what you're saying is that our poor little baby has got two equally stupid parents?'

'Afraid so, but we'll work it out between us.' Ben kissed her gently, before pulling away again. 'And we managed to get this business up and running, so that must prove we're not totally useless.'

'We've done okay, haven't we? And I can't wait to see what the Kings make of this place when they stay. I just hope there isn't anything we haven't thought of, and nothing goes wrong with their stay. If we start off with a bad review, my plan for converting the rest of the buildings might be over before it's even begun.' She looked around the room again. 'I think I should put some Christmas decorations up in here, to tie it in with the wedding theme.'

'Just don't give yourself more work to do, darling; they're going to love it anyway. And nothing's going to go wrong.'

'Promise?'

'I promise.'

Ellie leant into him again. There was no one in the world she trusted more than her husband, but she still couldn't shake off the sense of dread that something bad was about to happen.

3

Freya's mind was working overtime on the walk over to Le Debut. There had to be some way of finding out more about who her father was – her mother *must* have confided in someone. If it wasn't Auntie Linda, then who was it? Maybe her nanna had known. But if she had, then she'd taken the secret with her too. Maybe she should text her aunt, to ask if Linda could remember any of her mum's friends from around the time she'd fallen pregnant. Sophie, Freya's chief bridesmaid, would have been the first person she would have told if she'd found herself in similar circumstances. She might only have known her for three years, since Ollie had introduced them, but Freya could tell her anything. Her mother must have had a friend like that in her life – Freya was counting on it.

'Do you have a reservation, madam?' The maître d' greeted Freya with an expression which sent out the same sort of warning a guard dog might, but somehow he was smiling at the same time. She'd been to Le Debut often enough to know that you couldn't just turn up on the off-chance and get a table.

'A friend of mine is dining here, and I was planning to wait at the bar to meet him afterwards.' Even the house wine was over ten pounds a glass, so the irony of nursing one drink on a nurse's salary, until Ollie finished his business lunch, wasn't lost on her. And much as she was dying to tell him what she'd found out about her dad, there was no way she was going to interrupt his meeting. She'd already rushed over to her auntie Linda's place like a tornado and left her reeling. She couldn't put Ollie in that situation whilst he was at work. Now that she was actually here, a big part of her thought she should probably have done what she'd promised Jeremy, and headed home. But she was sure Ollie would understand why she *had* to tell him. He knew her better than anyone and he'd promised to love her forever. So he'd forgive her getting over-emotional and turning up unannounced; he was the kindest man she'd ever known – aside from her father – and it was just one of the things she loved about him.

Sitting at the bar with nothing to do but scroll through her phone and try to sip her wine as slowly as possible, Freya took the opportunity to text her aunt.

✉ Message to Auntie Linda
I hope I didn't upset you too much today and thanks for telling me what you know. I was wondering if speaking to Mum's friends might help, in case she confided in one of them? xx

Halfway through her first glass of wine, Freya's phone pinged.

✉ Message from Auntie Linda
I think most of your mum and dad's friends were people they got
to know after they got together, but I do remember one girl your
mum was close to back then. They went down to Kelsea Bay
together every summer. Her name began with an M, I think. I've
just texted Dave to see if he can remember more as he's much
better with names than me. Chin up lovey and I'll text you if
there's more to tell xx

Patience had never been Freya's number one virtue, but
waiting for her aunt to text back was testing it to the limit,
and she forgot all about the plan to slowly sip her drink. Ten
minutes later she was already halfway down the second
glass, a warm glow settling in her stomach, and the smell of
mulled cider drifting across from the other side of the bar
was becoming increasingly tempting. Another ten minutes
passed, and she'd just drained the last of the second glass of
wine, when her phone pinged again.

✉ Message from Auntie Linda
Good job Uncle Dave's got a better memory than me. Your
mum's friend was called Denise Johnson. Don't know where I
got the M from! Dave's going to help me look through Facebook
later to see if either of us recognise her, but chances are she'll
have changed her name. I'll keep in touch xx

Freya read the message twice, nerves suddenly fluttering
in her chest at the prospect of trying to track down a
stranger who might be able to tell her who her biological
father was. He probably hadn't told anyone the secret her
mother had kept from her either. There might be a very

good reason for that. Maybe he'd already been married when Freya was conceived and here she was planning to crash into a life he'd chosen to keep her out of. Her aunt had probably been right; the chances of this ending well weren't good and yet she already knew she wasn't going to be able to stop searching for him. At the very least she had to know if he was still alive, to see his face and say his name. If that was all she got from this, she could accept it. As long as she had Ollie, she could get through anything.

Freya ordered a glass of mulled cider from the barman, which slipped down even more easily than the wine had. Never mind waiting for Uncle Dave and Auntie Linda to start their detective work, she'd search for the name herself. There were hundreds of Denise Johnsons on Facebook, though, and there was no way of knowing if she still went by her maiden name – even if she was on there. It was just her luck that her mum's friend had a common name. Why couldn't she have been called something outlandish like December Cinnamon-Stick, anything to narrow the search down.

'December Cinnamon-Stick.' Freya giggled as she said the words out loud, earning a raised eyebrow from the barman, who was busy drying glasses, and had probably seen it all before. 'I think this cider's going to my head.'

'Can I get you something else, instead?' The barman gestured towards the coffee machine at the end of the bar, but she shook her head.

'I just need to nip to the loo, that's all.' She stood up. Her whole body seemed to have flooded with warmth, and her face felt more flushed than ever. Two large glasses of wine and half a pint of mulled cider, on an empty stomach, probably wasn't the best idea she'd ever had. She'd have to leave the car where it was, in the car park near Ollie's office, and pick it up the next day.

'There's a cracked pipe in the bar washrooms, I'm afraid. So, unfortunately, you'll have to use the restaurant facilities.' The barman furrowed his brow and Freya giggled again. There was something incomprehensibly funny about the way he'd said *facilities,* almost like it was a rude word.

'That will be fine, thank you.' For some reason, her attempt not to sound as tipsy as she felt had resulted in a very bad impression of the queen. Maybe she should order that coffee when she got back. Walking across to the heavy doors that separated the bar from the diners, she stepped into the restaurant. Not wanting to catch Ollie's eye by accident and risk him seeing her, and interrupting his meeting, she kept her head down. He'd have to walk out through the bar to exit the restaurant, so there was no way she could miss him leaving unless she happened to be in the washroom just at the wrong moment. She'd have to get back to the bar quickly, just to make sure.

Less than a minute later, she was in and out of the cubicle and staring at her reflection in the mirror as she washed her hands. Her cheeks were flushed red, just as she'd known they would be, but the rest of her face looked normal, exactly as it had that morning – before Ollie left for work, when she'd still been Colleen and John Halliwell's daughter. She still had her dad's nose, or what she'd always thought of as her dad's nose. Any likeness could now only be put down to the fact that they'd both broken their noses during their teens – her falling off a horse, and him on the rugby pitch. It was purely coincidental.

She definitely didn't want any more alcohol – it wasn't going to do her ability to search for Denise Johnson online any good. And it was in danger of making her melancholy and undoing all the good intentions she had after speaking to Linda – to see the search for her birth father as an opportunity. Her existence might not be a deep, dark secret after all. For all she knew, her biological father could just have been too young and overwhelmed to cope with the news that her mother was having a baby and he might have spent the last twenty-eight years regretting that. It could all be really different now and there was a good chance she had a brother or sister out there somewhere, maybe even two or three, and that was something she'd always wanted.

'Let me get that for you.' She'd been seconds away from going back through to the bar when she'd stopped to help the elderly lady in front of her, who was struggling to manage the heavy doors. Stepping backwards, her eyes automatically scanned the restaurant. And that's when she saw them – Sophie and Ollie, their heads so close together that they were almost touching, her hand reaching out for his. The intimacy between them was as obvious as the lie he'd told Jeremy about having a working lunch, and the even bigger lie he'd told Freya about not having time to stop for a break at all.

The shock of finding her mother's journal had sent her running to her aunt's house, but this time the shock seemed to have rooted her to the floor, and she couldn't take her eyes of her fiancé and his oldest friend, staring at each other, oblivious to the rest of the world, including Freya.

Sophie, her chief bridesmaid, and the friend who'd supported her almost as much as Ollie and his family had, when her mother had died. The same friend who'd helped her pick out everything for the wedding, from the dress to the menu, when Ollie had just said she should have whatever she wanted. *'As long as you're happy, I'm happy.'* Those had been his exact words, but all the time Sophie had been the one making him happy. A weird, guttural sound escaped from her lips, as she finally stepped towards them. She was almost close enough to reach out and touch Ollie by the time he spotted her, his head jerking back from Sophie's caress and his eyebrows shooting up in surprise.

'Freya.' His eyes darted from her face to Sophie's and back again. A few more bits of the puzzle were suddenly clicking into place. The times when Sophie had asked Freya if she was sure she wasn't rushing into getting married, and if it wouldn't be better to get settled in London first, so that it wouldn't be so stressful. To give her credit, she'd played the part of the concerned friend amazingly well.

'So you still remember my name then, Ollie? Despite it slipping your mind this morning that you had this cosy little lunch booked with Sophie, when you didn't even have twenty minutes spare to meet me.'

'It's not what it looks like.' Even Ollie had the grace to cringe, as Sophie trotted out the age-old cliché.

'So what exactly is going on then?' Turning to look at the woman she'd thought of as her best friend, almost since the moment they'd first been introduced, Freya was determined not to cry. Deep down she still couldn't believe that Ollie would cheat on her, but after what she'd discovered in her mother's journal, anything seemed possible. She thought they'd shared everything, and she thought she could trust Ollie with her life if she needed to. But if her mother could live a lie for all those years, what made Ollie any different? Especially when the evidence seemed to be stacking up against him.

Suddenly, Sophie's throwaway comments about missing the opportunity to be more than friends with Ollie, because they'd known each other since before they could talk, took on a whole new meaning. '*He's a great guy, but it would have felt weird. I love him, just not like that.*' She'd said it more than once and then laughed it off, but Freya would almost certainly have heard the regret in her voice if she'd really listened. Maybe she was just easy to deceive, or maybe she'd allowed herself to be because she wanted to live in the little bubble where everything had been simple and perfect. Either way, it was like everything she thought she'd known about her life had all come crashing down in one day.

'This is my fault, not Ollie's.' Sophie turned towards Freya, her face so drained of colour that it almost matched the white linen table cloth in front of her.

'What's your fault?'

'I just wanted to be sure... you know, that this was right for all of us.' Sophie dropped her gaze and Freya's fingers twitched, the desire to tip the bottle of sparkling water on the table over her bridesmaid's head, almost overwhelming.

'Funny that. I never realised there were *three* of us in this relationship. Silly me; all this time it was about all of us, not just the two of us.'

'Freya don't, I—' Ollie barely had the chance to open his mouth before she cut him off.

'Don't you dare! Whatever it is you're going to tell me to think or feel, just don't. You lied to Jeremy about having a working lunch, and you lied to me. What possible reason could you have for doing that?' She didn't wait for an answer, but a realisation was setting in like concrete. Whatever reason he'd had for lying, it didn't matter. Cheating had always been a deal breaker for both of them, he knew that, but suddenly lying for any reason was a deal breaker too. She'd been lied to for her entire life and she wasn't about to start a new life with someone who found it this easy to lie to her too.

'There's nothing going on, Freya. Sophie wanted to see me because she was struggling to accept that things are going to change when you and I get married. I was just trying to stop things getting awkward between the two of you. I didn't want this to affect your friendship, because it's only ever been you for me. You've got to believe me.' Ollie sounded desperate, but it was too late. He didn't have enough faith in her to trust her with the truth, even if he was being honest. No one in her family had had enough faith in her either. Freya was just someone who needed to be kept in the dark on the outside of every circle of secrets and there was no way she was going into a marriage like that, even if Ollie's reason for meeting Sophie had been totally innocent.

'I don't have to do anything. Not any more. How am I supposed to decide which lies to fall for, anyway?'

'I asked him to keep how I've been feeling a secret.' Sophie had no idea how little she was doing to help the situation every time she opened her mouth.

'And in doing that he chose *you*.' Freya's fingers twitched again, but this time she wasn't even tempted to tip the water over Sophie's head. She was vaguely aware that everyone else in the restaurant was looking at them, and she wasn't going to give them the satisfaction of making a scene.

Having her heart broken twice in the space of five hours was something she couldn't do anything about, and she might not be walking away with much, but she could at least try to hold on to her dignity. 'Enjoy your little club of two, sharing all your secrets, and don't worry there aren't three of us in this relationship any more, because I'm done.'

Dropping her engagement ring on the table, Freya spun around, but Ollie was up on his feet with his hand on her shoulder before she'd made it even halfway back to the doors that led out to the bar. She couldn't stop; if she did, everything might come bursting out – the discovery that her dad wasn't her birth father, and the true extent of just how badly her fiancé and her best friend had just broken her heart by lying to her too. Even if he hadn't physically cheated, the secrets felt every bit as painful of a betrayal. But Ollie had no right to even know about her mother's secret any more, and she'd do anything not to let either of them see her cry.

'Don't touch me.' It was a hiss and the people sitting closest to where Freya was standing weren't even pretending not to watch them now.

'Please Freya, I love you so much and I know I handled it badly, but I was just trying to protect you both. I didn't want to hurt her feelings, but I didn't know if you'd understand.'

'Nice to know that you prioritised Sophie's feelings over being honest with me. I said *don't touch me.*' Freya shrugged off his hand, as he tried to comfort her again. 'Conveniently enough, my stuff's already packed for the move, so I'll clear the flat by the weekend.'

'Are you seriously telling me you're ending everything over *this*? I should have told you, I know that now, but you can't let this break us up' He looked at her. 'We're getting married in a week and I love you far too much to let this happen, over an idiotic error of judgement on my part. I'll do whatever it takes to put this right.'

'We *were* getting married, you mean.' Freya bit her lip in a vain attempt to transfer the emotional pain into something physical. 'I don't trust you any more, Ollie. I've been lied to my whole life, and now it turns out you're lying to me too.'

'What do you mean you've been lied to your whole life? You're not making any sense.'

'It doesn't matter.' Freya didn't look him in the face. She hadn't meant for it to come out, but she couldn't think straight and she needed to get out of there before she told him far more than she wanted to.

'Something's happened, hasn't it? I know you, Freya, I can tell.'

'You might think you know me, but you don't. No one really does.' That was as much as she was going to give him, and the audience of diners hanging on their every word.

'Freya, please, whatever it is that's happened you can tell me. It's the reason you're overreacting to all of this.'

'Overreacting?' Freya's voice shook. The emotion was so close to bubbling over, if she didn't get out of the restaurant in the next two minutes she was definitely going to lose it. 'Do you know what, Ollie, I *have* got something to tell you.'

'What is it?'

'Goodbye.' Breaking into a run, Freya shot back through the bar and had almost reached the exit on to the street before the barman called out.

'Madam, your bill?'

'Just add it on to Ollie King's restaurant tab. He owes me.'

* * *

Uncle Dave puffed heavily as he carried the last of the boxes into the living room, stacking it on top of the others next to the white tinsel Christmas tree that Auntie Linda had covered with what looked like about a hundred strings of tinsel, all in brightly clashing colours. Freya's head was pounding so hard she couldn't even look at it.

'Did you see Ollie?' She turned to her uncle who nodded slowly. As well as collecting her stuff, Dave had dropped the car back to the flat. Ollie had a company car, but the one Freya had been using was registered in his name too, and she didn't want to give him any reason to come looking for her.

'He really wants to see you, to explain.' Dave shrugged. 'I didn't get half of what he was saying, he seemed so distraught, but I could tell the boy's genuinely heart-broken.'

'Don't let him fool you. He's proven just how capable he is of lying.' Freya hugged the cushion she was holding into her body.

'Are you sure he didn't have a point about you overreacting? With the day you've had, no one would blame you lovey.' Linda's tone was reasonable, but Freya shook her head so hard the pounding sensation seemed to double.

'I'm not, and you weren't there.' A tiny voice was nagging at the back of Freya's brain, that maybe there was something in what her aunt was saying. She'd played the scene over and over in her mind and it had definitely been Sophie leaning in towards Ollie with him patting her shoulder as if he was comforting her, rather than anything else. But she squashed the voice down again. She couldn't trust what she saw, or what she thought, because somewhere along the way she must have lost the ability to recognise the truth. Maybe it was something she'd never learned... She'd been lied to from almost the moment she was born, and she couldn't imagine ever really trusting anyone again.

'But moving all your stuff and cancelling the wedding...' Linda sighed heavily. 'There couldn't be a worse time for us to be heading off to Australia and leaving you here all on your own.'

'I'm not staying here.' Freya had made up her mind sometime in the haze of white-hot fury that had descended on her as soon as she'd left the restaurant. She'd had no idea where to turn and it had felt as if she'd been rejected from every safe haven she thought she had. Her closest family had lied to her and so had the man she loved. Where were you supposed to go from there? Much to her surprise, the threatened tears hadn't come. Instead, it had been like some unstoppable momentum had taken over, and within seconds she'd been making her first call to cancel collecting the wedding rings and her final dress fitting. Seabreeze Farm had taken over a lot of the arrangements, but she'd cancelled anything that hadn't been booked through them. They'd be losing a lot of their deposits, but the prospect of losing money barely registered. It was nothing compared to everything else she'd lost that day.

Galvanising Uncle Dave and some of his mates from the pub into action, had taken a bit more persuasion. Especially when Auntie Linda kept interrupting to say she was sure it would all blow over, and shouldn't Freya give it a few days before she started cancelling the wedding plans. The promise of a couple of rounds of drinks, after they helped out, had been enough in the end to get Dave's mates on side, and one of them had a transit van that was perfect for transporting the boxes she'd already packed. Another of her uncle's friends had even agreed to throw Freya's clothes and the contents of her dressing table into a couple of suitcases. If he didn't quite get it all, she could live with that, as long as she didn't have to face Ollie.

'What do you mean you're not staying here?' Auntie Linda knitted her eyebrows together, and Dave grunted again as he sat down on the sofa beside her.

'I'm not sure I can face moving all your stuff again just yet, sweetie. My back's not what it used to be.'

'I'm sorry, I shouldn't have asked you to do it, but I was desperate. You and Linda are all I've got.'

'Hey.' Dave reached across to the armchair where Freya was sitting and touched her hand. 'Of course you should have asked me, and I'd do anything for you, but I just can't face another removal yet.'

'I can't see why you'd have to.' Linda was running a hand through her hair as she spoke. 'I thought you staying here, and looking after the place whilst we're in Australia, would be the perfect solution. It'll give you time to think.'

'I don't need time to think.' Freya looked from Linda to Dave. 'But don't worry, I'm not going to ask you to move my stuff again. If I can leave that here, just until you get back from visiting Scotty, that would really help.'

'And what about you, where are you going to stay?' Linda's eyes searched her face and Freya tried her hardest to smile, even if she ended up feeling about as convincing as a shop mannequin.

'I know what I need to do and I've got a plan.'

'Are we allowed to know what this plan is?' Linda was going to end up pulling a tuft of hair out the way she was running her hand through it, and Freya resented Ollie even more for forcing her to involve her aunt and uncle in this. But there was no way she was going to let this ruin the trip to Australia they'd been planning for almost two years.

'I'm going to stay at an old friend's place over Christmas and decide whether I still want to take the job in London. Or if I should apply for something else, as far away from Ollie and Sophie as I possibly can.'

'What's her name, this old friend?' Uncle Dave had narrowed his eyes, as if he didn't quite believe her.

'It's Karen, but I'm not going to tell you where she lives because then Ollie might get it out of you and I know a part of you still thinks I should give him another chance. But that's not going to happen; I'm done with secrets and I'm struggling to cope with everyone else telling me how I should feel about them.' She held out her hands to both of them. 'I love you both, but I've got to do this for me. So much has changed, so quickly, and I just need time to process it all. On my own.'

'What do you mean "on your own"? What about Karen?' Auntie Linda's eyebrows had knitted back together again.

'I just mean without anyone who knows Ollie or Mum and Dad trying to influence me. I won't literally be on my own.'

'Good because I couldn't stand the thought of you being alone for Christmas.' Uncle Dave was built like the proverbial side of a barn, but his voice cracked as he looked at her again.

'I promise I won't be, and I promise I'll have everything

sorted out by the time you get back from Australia. But I need you to promise me something, too. I don't want you to tell Ollie what I found out about Mum, no matter how much he pushes you for information. He's got no right to know about any of that and, whatever you might think, my decision to call off the wedding has got nothing to do with finding out about my father.' Freya's tone was forceful and if there was a part of her that was trying to convince herself, as well as Dave and Linda, she wasn't going to acknowledge it.

'If that's what you really want, then we promise. But you won't do anything stupid, will you?' Auntie Linda suddenly looked so much like her mum, as she tilted her head on one side.

'Of course not. I'm all out of stupid anyway.' Freya forced another smile. If it had been stupid to trust the people who claimed to love her, then she'd been about as big a fool as she could be. She had to get away, and if that meant telling a lie of her own to the only two people she still trusted, despite everything, then it was a price she was willing to pay.

4

Freya glanced down at the Sat Nav on her new mobile phone, which she was using to track her taxi journey. They were already half way between the station in Kelsea Bay and Seabreeze Farm. No one knew where she was going, and only Auntie Linda and Uncle Dave had her new number, and that was only because they were going to Australia in a few days' time and had sworn on pain of death that they wouldn't give Ollie the number, whatever he said to them.

Freya had missed her mum every day since she'd died, but she'd never wanted to talk to her more than she did now. Not just to ask the obvious question about who her father was, but to talk about Ollie and Sophie. Linda had done her best, but it was obvious she still thought Freya had reacted too quickly. Her mother would have been 100 per cent on her side though – it was what mothers did – and she needed someone to believe she'd done the right thing. Especially as she'd woken up with a start, in the lumpy double bed in her aunt's spare room, terrified that she might have made the biggest mistake of her life.

She'd spent the rest of the night lying awake in the dark, longing for it to get light, and hoping that the old phrase about things looking better in the morning wouldn't just turn out to be a meaningless cliché. Weirdly enough it was true; the nagging doubt that had dogged her all night, might not have completely disappeared, but it was certainly less intense. The plan she'd made to go down to Kelsea Bay, and hide out there until after Christmas, didn't seem quite so crazy either. It had been Freya and her mum's special place and, over the years, they'd talked through hundreds of problems on the beach down there – everything from issues at school in the early years, to what her mother should do with the house after John had died. There'd been huge dilemmas and minor hitches, which Freya couldn't even recall by the following summer, but being able to use her mum as sounding board had made all the problems seem fleeting in the end.

In the last months of her life, her mother had told her more than once how glad she was that Freya had found someone like Ollie. He'd become her new sounding board, and they'd got through whatever problems crossed their path – together – just like Freya and her mum had always done. It was up to Freya now, though. She was on her own and she was going to have to get used to it. If she couldn't have her mum, then maybe walking on the beach in Kelsea Bay could work its magic instead. She had some huge decisions to make before New Year, and she was convinced that Kelsea Bay was the best place to make them.

* * *

Ellie lifted the lid of the casserole pot and poked the braising steak with a fork. She was no Nigella Lawson, but she was pretty sure the meat wasn't supposed to look grey. How had that even happened? There was the best part of a bottle of red wine in with it, as well as onions, mushrooms and a whole lot of seasoning. Recently she seemed to have developed an uncanny ability to turn good quality ingredients into something even the dog, Ginger, turned her nose up at.

'Ouch.' Ellie's grasp on the lid slipped, burning the tips of her fingers, as someone hammered on the farmhouse door. 'I'm just coming.'

'Hurry up, *please!*' The woman's voice sounded urgent, as Ellie got close enough to the front door to hear her. 'It's trying to attack me.'

Ellie stopped dead. She'd seen a documentary about gangs of burglars targeting rural properties, and there'd even been a case on *Crimewatch* the month before, where a farmer had been tied up and all his machinery stolen. Creeping forward, as the woman continued to shout, she looked through the coloured pane of glass, about two thirds of the way up the door. There was one woman out there, and she *was* being attacked – but only by two well-known reprobates, and Ellie was more than capable of handling them.

'I'm so sorry, I wasn't expecting anyone up at the farm today, so I put Gerald and Dolly out to eat whatever bits of winter grass they could still find around the yard. It saves getting the mower out.' Ellie ushered the woman inside, forgetting all about the prospect of a gang of farmyard thieves. 'They won't hurt you, though, they just can't resist seeing if there's anything in your pockets – even if that means almost knocking you flying!'

'It's my fault.' The mystery woman still had a look of panic in her dark brown eyes. 'I should have rung ahead, or taken the hint when the gate was locked, instead of climbing over it. But I was just so desperate to get here, and the taxi that brought me up from the station had already left. I wasn't expecting to find a donkey and a goat roaming loose, I must admit!'

'Like I said, I'm sorry about that, but I think you might have the wrong place. Were you looking for one of the holiday parks? Cliffside Cove is just up the road?'

'No. I definitely want Seabreeze Farm.'

'Oh God.' Ellie pulled a face. 'Please don't tell me I've forgotten a tour. The midwife warned me about baby brain, but I didn't realise I was going to be this bad.'

'Oh no, you aren't expecting me. At least not for another few days. I'm Freya Halliwell; my wedding was booked here for Saturday.'

'Oh my gosh, yes! I'm Ellie Hastings. My mum, Karen Crabtree, showed you around when you booked, didn't she?' Ellie smiled, relieved she hadn't forgotten an appointment. There were times since Karen's accident when she'd struggled to keep on top of everything, but forgetting a tour of the farm for a prospective bride would have been a new low. 'Did you need to drop something off for the wedding?'

'No.' Freya attempted a small smile, but then her chin wobbled. 'I need to cancel it.'

'Oh no.' Ellie wished Karen was there, but Alan had taken her to the hospital for some x-rays to check on her progress. Her mother always knew what to do in situations like this. Maybe it was because she was that bit older, or because of the things she'd been through with Ellie's father, but she had a way of comforting people and saying the right thing. Ellie just went into panic mode, trying to weigh up whether saying the wrong thing was better than saying nothing at all, until the silence was almost painful. 'Do you want to tell me why? I mean you don't have to, but—'

'It's okay. I can hardly cancel a wedding without telling people why, can I?' Freya was clearly still struggling not to break down.

'Why don't you come through to the kitchen and I'll put the kettle on, and you can tell me as much or as little as you want to.' Ellie ushered Freya along the corridor. 'And then we can work out the best way of cancelling everything.'

'So you can see why I wanted to cancel the wedding.' Freya looked down at the tea in front of her, which had gone cold whilst she was talking. She hadn't told Ellie the whole story, just the bit about finding Ollie and Sophie in enough of a compromising position to convince her that something was definitely going on, even if she still wasn't quite sure it was a full blown affair. She'd texted everyone from the contacts list on her old phone, to tell them the wedding was off, and put an announcement up on her social media accounts. It has been tempting to tell the whole world why the wedding was being called off, but the same need she'd felt at the restaurant, to retain a shred of dignity, over-rode any desire for revenge. In the end, it had taken her several attempts to word even a simple message.

Sorry for the late notice, but Ollie and I have decided to cancel our wedding this weekend. I won't be responding to any messages about this for the time being, but all gifts will be returned as soon as possible, and apologies again for any inconvenience caused.

After that, she'd chucked the SIM card from her old phone into the waste disposal unit in Auntie Linda's sink and deleted all the social media apps that had been pre-downloaded to her iPad. She wouldn't be adding any of the apps to her new phone, so anyone who wanted to contact her now might have to resort to carrier pigeon.

'Frankly I think he's lucky that calling off the wedding is all you did.' Ellie picked up her mobile. 'After all you've been through, I don't want you to be stuck paying out for any more than you have to, but there'll be some things we can't cancel at this stage without losing the deposit, and in some cases you might even have to pay in full. Things like the flowers and wedding cake are probably too late to cancel.'

'I'm not worried about that. We had an account, just for the wedding, that I set up with some of the money Mum left me when she died, so all of the bills can be covered. Although if someone else can make use of the flowers and the cake – maybe a local hospital or something – that would make me feel better than just wasting them.'

'I'm sure we can sort something out, but let me make some calls and see how bad the damage is first. It might not be too late to cancel some things.' Ellie was being so nice, it almost made it harder not to cry.

'I need to ask you one more favour.' Freya crossed her fingers under the table, hoping that one bit of luck would go her way. 'I know we didn't have The Old Stables booked until the night of the wedding, but I was hoping I might be able to rent it from today, if it's available?'

'It is! You were going to be our first guests.' Ellie gave her a sympathetic smile. 'So I don't see why not. If you're sure you still want to be here, when it's going to be so different to how you'd planned?'

'Thank you, that's brilliant, and I definitely want to be here. I need some time on my own to work out what's next and Kelsea Bay has always felt like a home from home.' Freya shoulders relaxed for the first time since she'd climbed over the gate and been chased across the farmyard by a donkey baring big yellow teeth that wouldn't have looked out of place on a piano keyboard. She'd expected The Old Stables to be fully booked until the wedding, and had looked up a couple of local hotels as a back-up plan. It was time to see if her luck would stretch any further. 'I don't suppose it's free for a bit longer than our original booking, is it? I'd like to stay on until Christmas if I can.'

'There aren't any other bookings until well into the New Year, as we wanted to leave ourselves times to sort out any issues after the first stay.' Ellie wrinkled her nose. 'Although I probably shouldn't admit that we were using you as guinea pigs.'

'I've been used as far worse.'

'I'm so sorry, I wish I knew what to say.'

'You don't have to say anything; sorting out the cancellations and letting me stay in The Old Stables is helping far more than you'll ever know.' A sense of calm descended on Freya, which she hadn't felt since the moment her mother's journal had dropped open on that fateful page. 'But there is one more thing you can do.'

'If I can, I will.'

'I don't want Ollie to know I'm here, or for anyone else who might tell him to find out. So, if anyone phones here asking about me or the wedding, please can you just tell them you don't know anything except that the wedding's cancelled, and that you definitely haven't heard from me?'

Ellie looked at her for a long moment, as if weighing up what she'd asked her to do. 'You said it was your bridesmaid you saw him with, didn't you?'

'Yes.' It felt weird every time she said it, like witnessing something you just couldn't believe was real and the memory was already hazy around the edges. The Ollie she'd known couldn't have been sitting there holding his oldest friend in his arms, like she meant the world to him, yet he had been.

'In that case, I don't think he deserves to know a single thing.'

'Thank you.' Freya smiled again, and for once she didn't have to force it.

5

Freya opened her eyes and for a moment she didn't know where she was. The twinkling fairy lights, strung from the beam above her head, came into focus as she sat up. It would have been a romantic place to spend a few nights after the wedding, and Ellie had done a great job of making The Old Stables look festive too. There was a six-foot potted Christmas tree, decorated with strings of ceramic ginger bread men, red and gold baubles, and more fairy lights. She'd planned to lie down on the huge king-size bed just for a moment or two, after Ellie had left her to get comfortable, but exhaustion had swept over her, and she'd slept right through until the next morning.

Standing up, she caught sight of herself in the full-length mirror positioned in the corner of the room. She was still wearing the clothes she'd travelled down in, and the crumpled sheets had left an imprint on her face. It wasn't a pretty picture. She had no idea what she was going to do with the day, but whatever it was, she wanted it to take her a step closer to finding her father. Before all of that, she needed a shower. Ellie had insisted on half-emptying her kitchen cupboards in the farmhouse to stock the kitchen in The Old Stables. So she had plenty of food, but more importantly she had coffee. That was two decisions she'd made already – to have a shower and a coffee – and maybe, after that, she'd remember why coming down to stay at Seabreeze Farm had seemed such a good idea.

It had been a knee-jerk reaction in some ways, but she hadn't wanted to lie to her aunt Linda, and she's met Karen during the tour of the farm. It meant that telling her aunt and uncle she was staying at Karen's place hadn't been a complete lie, and it had saved them worrying. There was nowhere else she could have gone that Ollie couldn't track her down to – he knew all her friends. That was if he even wanted to look for her. For all she knew, he could be making the most of his new found freedom to be with Sophie. And if he'd been telling the truth and there was nothing going on, he probably hated her anyway. When she missed him the most she tried to make herself picture the first option, Sophie draping herself all over him the way she had at the restaurant, but when she tried to summon the image she could never picture Ollie's face.

There were two fluffy robes hanging in the bathroom of The Old Stables, with the words *Mr and Mrs* embroidered on the back. Poor Ellie would be mortified that she hadn't remembered to whip them out with the other stuff. Freya had seen her scoop up some mugs with the same wording on, and pull down a string of wooden love hearts that had been hung above the bed. The clock on the wall seemed to be moving more slowly than any other clock she'd ever looked at, but Freya knew exactly how many hours it was until she and Ollie would have been married and she couldn't wait for that moment to pass.

It might seem crazy to go to the wedding venue alone, but heading to Kelsea Bay had been her only option. Now she was here, that closeness she'd felt to her mother brought her absence into even sharper focus. In the taxi, driving past the bay that gave the small coastal town its name, Freya had almost been able to picture her mum on the beach. Pulling up outside Seabreeze Farm, she'd felt exactly like the eight-year-old version of herself she'd been the first time her mother had brought her up to the donkey sanctuary. Ellie's mother had told Freya, when she'd looked around the farm before booking the wedding there, that it was her aunt who'd owned the donkey sanctuary. Over the years, Freya had visited the sanctuary several times with her mother, until it had closed down. They'd fantasised about buying the place themselves, if they ever won the lottery, and her mother had talked about going back there in her last days. Imagining walking on the beach together in Kelsea Bay, as the cancer swept Colleen away, had given them both comfort.

The sound of something dragging against the front door of The Old Stables almost made Freya drop her coffee. 'Mum?'

It was like every horror movie she'd ever seen, but she didn't really believe in ghosts, or signs from the other side, and it was far more likely to be the donkey and goat who'd tried to mug her on the way into the farm, looking to see if they could ransack The Old Stables, too. Ellie had told her she would put them back in their usual paddock, but she wasn't taking any chances. Moving towards the window she pushed it open, and stuck her head out far enough to look towards the door. There was no sign of anyone. Maybe her imagination was playing tricks on her, hearing things that weren't there. As Ellie had pointed out, she'd been through a lot in the last few days. It was just stress, that was all. Stepping back, she was just about to close the window when she spotted the little ginger dog, who'd been curled up under Ellie's kitchen table. And two seconds later the mystery of the dragging sound was solved, as it scraped its front paws down the door again.

'Go home little dog, I haven't got anything in here you'd want.' Freya had no idea what the dog was called, but it was probably hoping for a scrap of bacon and a bit of sausage left over from breakfast. It was out of luck, though – Freya had barely eaten since opening her mother's journal. 'Go on, go home!' The little dog looked up at her and cocked its head on one side, as if considering the request. Then it started pawing at the door again. She was going to have to take it back to the house.

'Stop, no, you're supposed to be going in the other direction!' Freya opened the door so she could bend down and pick up the little dog, but it was too fast for her, shooting between her legs and into The Old Stables. 'Come back, you little—'

The dog turned and looked again, before trotting towards her. Scooping it up, she fully intended to take it straight back over to the farmhouse, but, as she did, the dog nuzzled against her neck, and for some unfathomable reason, tears stung her eyes.

'All right, you can stay for a bit, but as soon as Ellie

calls your name, you're going back to the farmhouse, okay?' The dog had big brown eyes, like chocolate buttons, and such an intelligent look on its face that it was impossible to believe it didn't understand every word she was saying.

Half an hour later, Freya was on the sofa, with the little dog curled up on her lap, nuzzling at her hand every time she dared to stop stroking it. Maybe Ellie would let her take it down to the beach with her; it would be nice to have some company and it might stop her looking out for her mother around every corner in Kelsea Bay.

Her mobile buzzed. That was the good thing about only having one contact in her new phone: she knew who was calling without even having to look at the caller display. Auntie Linda.

'Oh, thank God. I had visions of you not answering your phone, and me having to phone the police and tell them you've gone missing!' Auntie Linda's words came out in a rush, as if she'd been holding her breath and waiting for Freya to answer.

'I'm fine. I'm at Karen's place, like I said.' Freya held her phone in her left hand, and crossed the fingers of her right hand to cancel out the lie she was about to tell. 'She's even decorated my room for Christmas, and you don't have to worry about me not having company.' The dog nudged her hand as she uncrossed her fingers. What did it matter if the company was of the four-legged variety? At least dogs didn't tell lies.

'Well, that's great and it's probably a good thing you haven't told me where you are, as I'd almost certainly have folded by now and spilled the beans to Ollie.'

'You've spoken to Ollie?' Freya stopped stroking the dog and earnt herself another nudge.

'He turned up here, yesterday, begging me to tell him where you were and saying that he just wanted the chance to explain.' Linda sighed. 'I think you should let him, lovey. Looking at him, I just can't believe he was doing that *sort of thing* behind your back. If you hadn't found out about your dad a couple of hours before, I'm sure you wouldn't have taken it so hard.'

'Taken it hard? The fact that my fiancé and my best friend were meeting secretly behind my back isn't nothing. And Sophie's been trying to stop the wedding for ages, I just didn't realise until I saw them together.' Freya couldn't keep her voice steady, and the dog had its head cocked on one side again. 'I suppose I must have gullible stamped on my forehead, after the way I was brought up.'

'Don't, lovey. It would break your mum's heart to hear you talking like this; she only ever wanted to protect you. I couldn't believe how much she changed when you came along, from dreaming of seeing her name in lights, to giving her all to being your mum. If keeping that secret was a mistake, I bet you can count on one hand the number of other mistakes she made as a mother.'

'I can't think of any others, but the one she did make was pretty big.' Freya screwed her eyes shut; crying wasn't going to solve anything. 'I just wish I could talk to her and make sense of it all.'

'I can't wave a magic wand and make that happen; I only wish I could. But your uncle Dave has found the Denise Johnson we were after, except her name is Newman now. He was on the computer half the night searching through Facebook.' Linda tutted. 'His eyes were so bloodshot this morning he looked as if he'd had a heavy night on the drink.'

'How on earth has he found her with a different name?' Freya didn't want to let herself get too fixated on what Denise Johnson might be able to tell her. She had to be prepared for it being a dead end, because if she built up her hopes and got let down again she didn't know how she was going to pick herself up and carry on. Finding her father and maybe even a whole new family felt like the only light at the end of a very dark tunnel, but there were no guarantees that she'd ever get that far.

'Turns out your uncle Dave is a dab hand at a bit of detective work, bless him. He's been going around all morning telling me he should have been a detective inspector.' Linda laughed. 'I think it's a case of watching too many old episodes of Inspector Morse myself, but he found a Facebook group for the Kelsea Bay Yellow Coats.'

'Yellow Coats?' Freya's head still felt groggy from too much sleep, but none of this was making any sense.

'You remember your mum worked for one of the holiday parks in Kelsea Bay before you were born?'

'Yes.'

'Their entertainment team were called the Yellow Coats, as a blatant rip off of Butlin's red coats. Your uncle Dave always said they were the poor man's version, for Butlin's rejects, but never in front of your mum of course!'

'I remember watching re-runs of *Hi-de-Hi* when I was about eight and asking Mum if that's what she'd done for a job before she had me.' Freya could picture her mum now, in the photograph that had hung on the hallway wall, laughing with a group of other Yellow Coats as if she didn't have a care in the world.

'She always loved singing, your mum, and when she got her first summer season down in Kelsea Bay, she was so excited. She and Denise did everything together and they were convinced it was going to be their first step on the road to stardom. It was her third season down there when she fell pregnant with you.'

'I never realised she was so serious about it. I knew she loved singing, but I don't remember her ever performing in front of an audience. Singing "Somewhere Over the Rainbow" to me at bedtime was the closest she got.'

'And she'll have loved doing that more than anything.' Auntie Linda's tone was gentle. 'But there was a time when she and Denise had dreams of being the next big thing; she even refused to go by the name Colleen because it wasn't glamorous enough, so she used her middle name when she was performing.'

'Alannah?' Freya had never known any of those things. And it was difficult to equate the woman who'd seemed born to be a mother, and who everyone had called Coll, with this ambitious young singer. Other than the photograph in the hallway, there'd been no clue to her past life in anything she did or said.

'Yes, and your uncle Dave remembered that Denise called herself Dee Dee. I'd forgotten about that until he mentioned it. All that stuff seems like several lifetimes ago now.'

'I wish there were some more photos; I'd like to have seen that side of her.'

'I think she threw most of them away when she started

her new life with John, but I sent a box of old photos out to Scotty a couple of years back, because Jen was doing a photo wall in their living room and she wanted more photos from our side of the family. Maybe there'll be something in there.'

'That would be amazing.'

'You'd laugh your head off at some of the get ups they used to wear! They were obsessed with Kylie Minogue at the end of the eighties, and she had all this curly blonde hair piled up on top of her head in one of her music videos. So they went out, got perms and bleached their hair the exact same shade of blonde.' Linda paused for a moment. 'I used to take the mickey out of them, but I suppose deep down a part of me was jealous. They were always convinced they were about to get spotted, and there I was, working in the Co-op, and already married with a kid. My life seemed a bit grey in comparison.'

'But then an unexpected pregnancy came along and ruined all her plans.' Freya bit her lip. Until a couple of days before, she'd always believed she was a longed for only child, the miracle baby her parents had feared they might never have. That's what they'd told her, and it was amazing how much of her identity had been wrapped up in that story. She hadn't known just how much, until it had all been stripped away by a few words in a decades-old journal.

'You might have been unexpected, but you were the love of her life from the moment you came kicking and screaming into the world. I should know, I was there when you were born.'

'You were?' It was yet another revelation, but then Freya had never thought to ask about the details of her birth.

She'd just assumed that her dad had been the one holding her mum's hand through all of that.

'Yes, your nanna couldn't face it, and of course your biological father wasn't around, so I willingly volunteered. It was the second most amazing thing I've ever seen, because when I was having Scotty, I was in so much pain I couldn't take it in. I just wanted it all to be over!'

'What's the *most* amazing thing you've ever seen, then?'

'Your mum's face when she looked at you for the first time. So don't you ever think she didn't want you!'

'Thank you.' Freya's voice was barely more than a whisper, but she'd needed to hear those things. It was stupid, but she felt as if she'd let both her mother and John down in some way, by not being John's biological daughter. It was something that was totally out of her control, but her parents had obviously wanted to pretend she was John's child in every sense and she wished with all her heart it had been true. But she hadn't been able to grant the parents who'd given her so much that one wish. And now there was a drive inside her that she seemed to have just as little control over; a determination to find the father who'd played no part in her life and had already rejected her once. She was letting her parents down again and betraying John by wanting to find this other father, but it was a compulsion. She had to know who this man was.

'Your uncle Dave's the one you should be thanking. Not only did he manage to find Denise in that Facebook group, but he's also sent her a message, asking her to get in touch about your mum. If Coll confided in anyone about who your father is, then it will be Denise. I'm sure of it.'

'I hope so. Thanks again, and tell Uncle Dave he's still

my favourite uncle.' Freya's hand was shaking; there was so much riding on this, but she was incredibly grateful for her aunt and uncle's support.

'He's your only uncle!'

'Maybe not for much longer.' Freya took a deep breath, trying to imagine how it might feel to discover not just her father, but a whole extended family. She couldn't do it, though. It was like trying to envisage what was at the edge of the known universe, and it made her head hurt just thinking about it. One step at a time, that was the only way to handle this.

'We're off to do some more Christmas shopping to get the last few bits to take over to Scotty's, and I'll ring you as soon as there's any more news.' Auntie Linda hesitated again. 'But promise me you'll have a think about talking to Ollie. What harm can it do? And there's still time to go ahead with the wedding, if you can sort it all out. It's a couple of days away yet.'

'It's too late, everything's cancelled. And even if it wasn't, I could never be with someone I knew was capable of lying to me the way he did. Not after all of this.'

'Just think about it.' Auntie Linda wasn't going to give up. But there was more chance of the dog that was still nudging her hand – a scruffy, little terrier-cross with a coat like a broom-head – winning Crufts, than there was of her contacting Ollie. It was too late and the past couldn't be undone even if she wanted it to be. Her mother and John had spent their whole married life trying and she wasn't even going to consider following their lead.

* * *

'If I've got any post-baby weight to lose after working like this every day, then the world is definitely not playing fair.' Ellie hauled the bale of hay off the rack on the front of the quad bike, and started dropping pads of it onto the soft muddy ground in the paddocks where the winter grazing had all but disappeared. Talking to the animals had become a habit in the time since she and her mother had taken over the farm. Ben had caught her doing it several times in the early days of them getting together, but fortunately he was every bit as animal mad as she was. They were lucky to have found each other, in a world where so many people didn't seem to have what they did – a fact that had hit home more than once since they'd started running a wedding venue. There was the bride who'd had to have two ceremonies, because she couldn't have her divorced parents in the same room at the same time, and the groom who'd handed his number to one of the waitresses, 'just in case things didn't work out'. It could be depressing if you let it. But there were more than enough couples who looked like they'd found their *happily ever after* to balance it out. And then there was Freya, currently holed up in The Old Stables, nursing a bruised ego and a broken heart.

'Do you think I should go and see if she's okay?' Ellie addressed Gerald, her favourite of all the donkeys that were seeing out their days on the farm. He chewed a mouthful of hay and looked at her thoughtfully, as if he might be about to venture an opinion, but then he dropped his head to gather up another mouthful of hay. 'Yep, you're right, I should give her some space and I need to find Ginger anyway; there's a danger she'll get as bad as Holly for disappearing if she carries on like this. The last thing we need on the farm is another Houdini doing regular disappearing acts.'

Walking over to check the old bathtub that had a new lease of life as a water butt for the donkeys, Ellie breathed a sigh of relief. There was still plenty of water and she wouldn't have to bring a fresh supply down from the nearest tap a bucket at a time. It was one of her least favourite jobs even when she wasn't heavily pregnant and if Ben, Karen or Alan saw her doing it, they'd have something to say too.

'Hello sweetheart, how are you settling in?' Ellie patted the neck of the black donkey who'd sidled up to her in the hope of being given an extra treat of two. Jubilee had been retired early from her life as a seaside donkey in Lancashire, after a persistent leg injury meant she'd become just another mouth to feed for her owner. Ellie hadn't been able to resist offering her a home when she'd heard about Jubilee, even though she was one more mouth to feed amongst the many at Seabreeze Farm too. Giving a home to animals who needed one was Aunt Hilary's legacy, and Ellie was turning out to be an even softer touch than her great aunt. Jubilee had apparently been born on the day of the Queen's Golden Jubilee in 2002 and she could adopt a suitably regal expression when the mood took her. She had a lovely fluffy black coat and her nose felt like velvet under Ellie's hand, but she was still a bit nervous around Gerald and the rest of the donkeys. 'It's all right girl, you'll get used to these ruffians before long and you'll learn to love them, I promise.'

Ellie put the last of the hay in with the donkeys and got back on the quad bike. Once she'd found where Ginger was hiding out, she'd sort out some breakfast for her mum and knock back her third shot of Gaviscon for the day. Raging indigestion was just one more thing she wouldn't miss about being pregnant.

'Ginger! Ginger! Where are you girl?' Parking the quad bike under the cover of the open-sided hay store, Ellie did a circuit of the yard on foot, searching for the little dog. Ben had fed her and let her out before he'd headed off to work, but she hadn't seen her since. Normally she was Ellie's shadow, following her around in the hope that she might be given a little titbit to tide her over until her food bowl was filled up again. The only time she usually left Ellie's side was when Karen was cooking up a storm, and there was a good chance that something tasty might drop on to the kitchen floor. 'Come on girl, I honestly don't think I can chase around all morning looking for you any more.'

There was still no sign of her, and Ellie had just turned back towards the farmhouse, in case Ginger had snuck back into the kitchen, when she heard the scream. There was only one person in the house...

'Mum!' Ellie flung open the front door and ran down the hallway to the sitting room where her mother spent most of the day. She could still only get out and about in a wheel-chair and Ellie couldn't manage to push it over the gravel outside the farmhouse, or the rough ground beyond it. Alan and Ben both took her out when they could. But with both of them out working, Karen was slowly going stir crazy, and Ellie guessed what she'd done before she even saw her.

'I was just trying to get up, I'm so fed up with being useless and relying on everyone else to do the smallest things for me. I thought if I could get going on the crutches, I could be of more use. I'm sorry, sweetheart.' Karen was on the ground, the plaster cast forcing one leg out straight and the other one was curled underneath her. She was holding her right wrist with the opposite hand, and her cheeks were flushed red.

'The doctor told you not to try that without someone on hand to help.' Ellie fought the urge to shout at her. She'd have been every bit as impatient in her place, but it was hard to take care of someone who didn't seem to realise the importance of taking care of herself. 'Are you okay?'

'I think so. My right wrist is a bit sore where I tried to stop myself falling, but I don't think it's broken.'

'Oh God, I hope not. Let's get you up.' Ellie tried sliding her arms through her mum's, to haul her back into the chair, but even if her bump hadn't been doing such an amazing job of getting in the way, she'd never have been able to lift her mother. She was a dead weight and, once the full-length plaster cast was added to the equation, it just wasn't going to happen.

'You're going to hurt yourself.' Karen pushed her away with her good hand, sharpening her tone. 'I got myself into this mess and I'll just have to sit it out until Alan or Ben get back. It's not going to kill me to stay down on the floor.'

'Don't be ridiculous, Mum, you can't sit there all day.' Ben was out on a visit to his old friend Julian's for the whole morning, and the phone signal up there was notoriously bad. So he'd be unlikely to pick the message up before lunch time. Alan was out at a farmer's market, an hour's drive away, and he'd go into a frenzy of panic if Ellie called him in any case. She'd have to think of something else.

'I'm too heavy for you to get me up, and I'd never forgive myself if it hurt you or the baby trying.' Karen still sounded determined. 'Just pass me down a couple of those cushions and I'll be fine.'

Shaking her head, Ellie put one cushion behind Karen's back, to stop the footrest of the wheelchair sticking into it. 'I'll go and see if Freya's up to give me a hand; we should be able to lift you between us. Just don't move.'

'Like I've got any choice.' Karen pulled a face, but Ellie could see the relief in her eyes. She just hoped Freya would be able to help.

Ellie half-ran and half-waddled back across the farmyard to The Old Stables, hammering on the door in much the same way as Freya had done on the farmhouse door the day before.

'Ellie, is everything okay?' Freya was still in her pyjamas, but at least the mystery of where Ginger had disappeared to was solved. The little dog poked her head out of the door, clearly weighing up her options.

'I'm really sorry to have to ask this, but Mum's had a fall and she can't get up. I've tried to help her, but I can't do it on my own.' It was hardly the way to make a good impression with their first guest, but Ellie was out of ideas.

'Oh, no, is she okay? Of course I'll help.'

'She put her wrist out to stop herself falling, and she was holding on to it with her other hand. She says she's okay, but—'

'Don't worry, we'll get her up and I'm sure she'll be fine.' Freya didn't even stop to put on shoes, and Ellie saw her wince as she picked her way across the gravel in a pair of woolly bed socks.

'Do you want to go back and get something on your feet? She'll be fine for a few minutes.'

'It's okay, we're halfway there now, and I'd like to check your Mum over as soon as possible.' Freya must have spotted the confused look on her face and offered an explanation. 'I'm a nurse, so I can give her the once over, and then you can decide if you want to call an ambulance or anything.'

'I'm hoping she's not doing her classic thing of under-playing it and hasn't hurt herself badly. Although you can never tell with Mum.' Even as she'd been lying with her leg twisted at a horrible angle after the original fall, she'd kept saying it was probably just a sprained ankle. Her bravado had definitely been for Ellie's benefit, though, because she'd admitted later that she'd heard the crack of the bones breaking when she fell. God knows what she'd done this time, but Ellie tried not to panic as Freya followed her down the hallway and into the sitting room.

'If you wanted a bit of company you only had to say.' Freya was instantly reassuring, in the way the best medical staff always were. 'Let's get you back up in the chair and then we can check you haven't ruined your chances of making the Olympic volleyball team by damaging your wrist.'

'I've never been able to catch a ball, let alone volley one. I suppose they'd call it dyspraxia these days, but in my day they just called me a clumsy clot.' Karen smiled as Freya moved her good leg slightly.

'You need to learn to play catch with this new grandchild of yours, so you'd better get that wrist checked out.' Freya signalled to Ellie to move to the other side of her mum. 'Karen's leg is in the best position to get her up now, so if you can put your right arm under hers on that side and lift back-wards when I say so, we should be able to get her into the chair.'

'Okay.' Ellie felt the adrenaline begin to drain out of her. Here was someone who knew what she was doing, and most of the worry had subsided as soon as Freya took over.

'Right, here we go... one, two, three and up.' Both of them heaved Karen upwards and then back into the chair, a resounding thud sounding out when her bottom made contact with the seat.

'Oh thank you, girls. I'm so sorry, I've probably made you pull muscles you didn't even know you had.' Karen shook her head. 'But I won't be doing that again in a hurry.'

'Never mind worrying about us – are you okay?' Freya raised her eyebrows.

'I'm fine, I'm fine.' Even as Karen tried to brush them off, she was wincing and Ellie looked down at her mother's wrist. It was obviously swollen, a bruise already starting to spread across the skin.

'That wrist is broken, isn't it?'

Freya met her gaze. 'It's hard to tell just by looking. It could be a fracture, but a bad sprain can have pretty much the same symptoms, and sometimes the pain levels are higher for a sprain than a break. I think you're going to need an x-ray, Karen.'

'We'll have to call an ambulance.' Ellie recognised the look that flashed across her mother's face. *Over my dead body* just about summed it up.

'We can't call an ambulance out for a broken wrist.' Karen was shaking her head in a way that offered no argument.

'I can't get you into the car, Mum, not even with Freya's help.' Ellie hadn't thanked her yet for what she'd done so far, but she was already hatching a plan that might go some way to paying her back.

'I can just wait until Ben or Alan get home, and one of them can take me down to the hospital in the van. I'm not going to die of a broken wrist.' If Karen could have crossed her arms, she probably would have done. Alan had built a portable wooden ramp that they used to wheel Karen – wheelchair and all – into the back of the van he usually used for taking produce to the farmers' market. He'd even fashioned a seat belt of sorts, which he'd taken off the abandoned seat of an old tractor. Ben's van didn't have the same facilities, but Ellie got the feeling her mother would have been happy to be loaded onto a half-back truck, if it meant she didn't have to call an ambulance out.

'We should just call an ambulance, shouldn't we?' Ellie looked to Freya for support.

'If it looked like a compound fracture, or if I was worried it might be affecting the blood supply in any way, then I'd say yes.' She gave Ellie an apologetic shrug. 'But as it is, I think we'll be okay to wait. We can ice it for the swelling, and then I can dress it to keep any potential fracture stable, until she gets it looked at.'

'You see.' Karen widened her eyes. 'Freya knows what she's talking about; she told me all about her nursing when I took her around the farm in March. If we call an ambulance out, it means there's one less available for someone with a genuine emergency. It's bad enough that I've had to do that once already this year.'

'You mean when your leg was on a ninety-degree angle to where it should have been?' Ellie shook her head, knowing she was fighting a losing battle. 'I'll get some ice, the first aid kit, and maybe a strong cup of tea. Anyone else want one?'

By the time Ellie came back, resting the tray with the emergency kit and a pot of tea on top of her bump, Freya had elevated Karen's wrist and repositioned the foot rests on the wheelchair, so that she could rest her leg out in front of her and would stand absolutely no chance of trying to get up again.

'Freya has just been telling me why she called the wedding off.' Karen squeezed Freya's arm with her good hand. 'I could swing for that ex-fiancé of yours if I had enough limbs that were still working.'

'Thank you for not telling your mum what I told you. To be honest, when I mentioned it, I expected Karen to already know. Most people would definitely have passed that sort of gossip on.' Freya smiled at Ellie, as she set the tray down.

'It's not my business who to tell. I just let Mum know that the wedding was off and that you'd split up with your fiancé. The rest is for you to share, or not. Although I did warn her not to say anything to Ollie about you being here, which is just as well because he rang this morning.'

'Ollie rang here?' It was hard to gauge from Freya's reaction how she really felt about that information. The first look that had crossed her face had been almost hopeful, but then she'd frowned and folded her arms across her chest, as Ellie nodded. 'What did he want?'

'Just to know if I'd heard from you and, when I said I hadn't heard anything from you apart from your request to cancel the wedding, I could hear how disappointed he was. I think it's starting to dawn on him what he's lost.'

'Thank you for not telling him that I was here.' Freya

breathed out. 'I don't think I could face him yet and I'm hoping I won't ever have to. There's nothing to bind us together now.'

'I hate the thought of you sitting alone in The Old Stables and thinking about all of this.' Karen shook her head. 'Especially at this time of year, when you should be with your family, but if you ever need someone to talk to, it doesn't matter how late, you can always call one of us. Can't she Ellie?'

'Absolutely.' Ellie might be in bed by 9 p.m. most evenings these days, but her mother was right; the idea of Freya sitting alone and being overwhelmed by sadness was unbearable.

'Thank you both so much.' Freya smiled and gestured towards Karen. 'Although that could be dangerous because she has ways of making you talk, you know.'

'Oh, I do! I've never really been able to keep a secret from her as result. It makes buying presents a nightmare.' It was Ellie's turn to smile as she rested a hand on her bump. 'But I'm holding on to this year's big Christmas secret so far.'

'My mum was like that; I could never keep a secret from her either.' Freya's smile faded and Ellie stomach seemed to tie itself in a knot. Freya had told her the day before that she'd chosen Seabreeze Farm for the wedding, in memory of her late mother who'd loved Kelsea Bay. It was heart breaking enough that she was here because she'd called off her wedding, but being surrounded by reminders of her late mother must be making it even harder.

'We mothers like to give our opinions as well as getting you to spill your secrets.' Karen exchanged a look with her daughter. 'I was telling Freya about what your father put me through and how I'd put up with it all again ten times over to end up with Alan.'

'That's so lovely.' Freya began applying the ice to Karen's wrist as she spoke. 'But I don't think it'll ever happen for me.'

'Oh, I'm sure that's not true. I've never seen Mum as happy as she's been since Alan came into her life.' Ellie tore off the plastic around the bandage she'd taken out of the first aid kit. 'And at least you didn't have a child with your ex before you found out what he was really like. Trust me, having a dad like that is worse than having no dad at all.'

'Oh sweetheart, what is it?' Karen turned towards Freya as she started to sob. And if she hadn't been heavily pregnant, Ellie would have kicked herself in the leg. How did she always manage to do this, even when she was setting out with the best of intentions? Freya had seemed a hundred times more together than she had been the day before, until Ellie had gone and opened her big mouth.

'I'm sorry, it's not you, it's just my dad. I...' Freya took a deep breath, looking from Karen to Ellie and back again. 'The same day that I found out Ollie had been meeting our bridesmaid behind my back, I found out that the man I'd always called dad wasn't my father at all.'

'Oh love.' Karen put her good arm around Freya and pulled her close. 'You don't have to tell us any more if you don't want to, but you've been through so much and if it helps at all to talk about it, I've got all the time in the world to listen.'

'You've already helped, more than you know. But actually I think I would like to talk about it, if you're sure you don't mind? It might help me get it straight in my head, because I still can't seem to make any sense of it on my own.' Freya turned her head and Ellie managed a small nod. Ten minutes later they knew as much as Freya did about who her father was. And Ellie was determined to help her, to repay what Freya had done for Karen, even if that meant getting every last person in Kelsea Bay involved.

6

The morning dawned bright and crisp on what would have been Freya's wedding day. There was still no news from her mum's old friend, Denise, according to Auntie Linda, but at least she'd stopped nagging Freya to make contact with Ollie. Once any chance of reinstating the wedding plans had passed, it finally seemed to sink in that the break-up was real, and not just an overreaction to discovering her mother's secret.

She'd been due to spend the night before the wedding by herself at The Old Stables, to honour the tradition of the bride spending one last night apart from the groom, so when a package arrived at the door addressed to her, early in the morning, Freya worried that Ollie had worked out where she was. But the delivery note in the bottom of the outer box made it clear that the request for the package to arrive on that date had gone in two weeks before she'd confronted Ollie and Sophie in the restaurant.

Inside the plain brown package was a beautifully

wrapped gift box, and inside that was a small velvet box in the deepest navy blue. Opening it, Freya caught her breath. It held what was clearly a vintage gold locket, the marks of wear and tear somehow making it all the more beautiful. She knew what would be inside before she even opened it – a tiny version of Freya's favourite picture of herself and her parents, taken on the day they'd played Undercover Santa, not long before her father had died. There was a note inside the gift box too, but it took Freya almost twenty minutes to decide whether or not she wanted to read it. In the end, she couldn't resist.

> *My darling Freya. I know you'll be missing your parents more than ever today and I hope this helps you feel they're close by. When I saw the locket, I knew I had to buy it because it was so you. Hearts that have been hurt are so much stronger than they realise and they're the most beautiful too. I can't wait to be your husband and I promise I'll spend the rest of our lives protecting your heart. All my love, Ollie xxxx*

Words, that was all they were. Anyone could come up with a corny line or two that promised the earth. She might have fallen for it before and Freya knew herself well enough to admit she'd have been thrilled with the gift if the wedding had been going ahead, because it really was perfect. Ollie had known her well too, though, and he'd always been able to say just the right thing. But that was all in the past. Dropping the box back into the velvet box, she snapped it shut. If Ollie's idea of protecting her heart was to lie to her face, then maybe he hadn't ever really known her at all.

She spent the rest of the morning keeping as busy as possible, having coffee with Karen on the pretext of making sure she was recovering okay, from what had thankfully turned out to be a badly sprained wrist. She'd offered to run a few errands for Ellie and Karen too, and at first they'd seemed reluctant to accept the offer of help, but when she'd confessed that it would help to keep her mind off things, they'd suddenly reeled off a list of jobs she could do. Feeding the donkeys had been a particular highlight and even Gerald, who'd chased her across the farmyard on the day she'd arrived, looked as gentle as a lamb from the other side of the fence. Jubilee was her favourite, though. The little black donkey had such a wise and thoughtful expression on her face and she stood away from the rest of the donkeys, as if she was trying to protect herself from the risks of getting too involved. It was definitely something Freya could identify with.

Leaning on the gate and watching them, just for a moment it had felt like her mum was standing alongside her. Carrying buckets of water from the tap to the troughs in the paddocks was far harder work, but it did a pretty good job of stopping her thinking about what she would have been doing, had the wedding still been going ahead. At around the time she would have been getting her hair done, she was helping Ellie round the chickens back up into the coop, and she had a feeling that her new friends had known exactly what they were doing when they'd given her such a long list of jobs.

Much as she was grateful for everything Ellie and Karen had done, she needed to be alone at three o'clock when the ceremony would have started. She didn't want to sit inside

The Old Stables, though, watching the twinkling fairy lights that seemed to mock her with their relentless cheerfulness. Ginger, whose name she'd finally discovered after she'd bandaged Karen's wrist, seemed to have more or less taken up residence with her, and Ellie didn't seem to mind. Walking the dog every day was another task she'd taken on, and it meant she'd have some company at three o'clock, too – the perfect sort of company, where she wasn't required to utter a single word.

It was the first day she hadn't spent every five minutes checking her phone. There was still no response from Denise and she couldn't just sit around and wait for one. Finding out about her father had been the catalyst for Freya's future imploding, and if her new future didn't involve finding him, then she had no idea what it would involve. If she was going to stand any chance, she'd have to take up where her uncle had left off. There was a chance Denise wouldn't ever respond to the message, but she'd try every single member of the Kelsea Bay Yellow Coats Facebook group until someone did. She'd started by searching through the posts in the group and finding a copy of the picture her mother had hung in their hallway. Almost everyone in the photograph had been tagged and they were the first people she'd messaged.

Freya hadn't been content with leaving it all in the lap of Facebook and she'd spent hours searching through the online archives of the *Kelsea Bay News* for old articles about the Yellow Coats. She'd found quite a lot of stories and photos from the years when her mum had been a member of the team. Zooming in on blurry images, she'd tried to spot someone else she might recognise, a facial feature or expression that might somehow reveal who her father was. But there was no blinding moment of revelation. She'd then decided to start compiling a list of names of Yellow Coats who weren't in the Facebook group and tried to work out how on earth to track them down. For one day all of that could wait, though, she just had to get through another nine hours and the wedding day that never was would finally be over.

It was quite a long walk down into Kelsea Bay, but Ginger was still pulling excitedly on the lead by the time they reached the beach. As she unclipped the dog's collar, as they reached the edge of the sand, it was as though someone had fired a starting pistol and Ginger was in the race of her life. She shot across the sand, flicking it up as she turned in circles and chased after a seagull that she was never going to catch. It was twice the size of her anyway, but the thrill was obviously all in the chase. Maybe that's how it had been with Ollie, and when marriage had suddenly poked its head around the corner it had lost all its thrill. She blew out her cheeks and then let go, trying to breathe out all thoughts of Ollie at the same time. It was what all the self-help websites recommended, that and meditating, but none of the techniques she'd read about seemed to be fulfilling their promises. Karen had told her that the hurt of losing Ollie couldn't be avoided, she just had to ride the storm and get through it, filling her days and holding on until eventually the pain wasn't so bad any more. *Fake it until you make it*, was how Ellie had summed it up, and their advice seemed far nearer the mark than anything she'd read online.

Just walking seemed to help too. Winter was definitely in the air and there were sparkles of frost beginning to bind clumps of sand together, as the day drifted into evening. Tomorrow would be the start of a new life. There'd be no more thinking: *'in two days I would have been getting married'*, and eventually she might even forget the date itself. It seemed impossible now, but stranger things had to have happened.

'Come on, Ginger, we'd better get off the beach before it gets completely impossible to see.' It was almost five now and already dark, the lights on the promenade looking inviting as Freya walked back across the sand, with Ginger following close behind. Clipping the lead on to the dog's collar, they turned right towards the town itself. The houses that faced out on to the bay were all quite large, and lights were coming on in the windows as people started to arrive home from work. There were some houses with wreaths on the front doors, or lights strung from the balconies that offered a view of the bay. Lots of them had Christmas trees in their front windows as well, and there was something infinitely cosy about the glow of a light on the opposite side of a pane of glass, especially on a crisp winter's evening. Imagining the sort of people who might live in the houses was helping to distract her, too. What did the people with the fresh holly wreath think of their neighbours – the ones with the family of snowmen, which burst into song when someone walked by? One thing she knew for sure was that her auntie Linda would have loved them.

The high street in Kelsea Bay was one of those rare places which was still mostly filled with little independent shops and cafes, and it was also famous for miles around for taking its Christmas lights display very seriously. Although Freya and Colleen had visited every summer for at least a week without fail, they'd also driven all the way over from Bristol for a weekend in December, a handful of times. Freya's favourite shop had always been Driftwood Island. In the summer, the window display was filled with all sorts of seaside themed gifts, hand-crafted from local materials. She still had a family of seagulls that had been hand-carved from driftwood washed up on the beach in Kelsea Bay itself, which her mother had bought her the summer before she'd headed off to university to study for her nursing degree. There'd been three seagulls of various sizes, standing side by side on a rock, and her mum had said it was just like the three of them, their own little family. It was hard not to think of a million conversations with changed meanings, now that she knew the truth about her dad, or at least half the truth.

On the occasions when they'd visited Kelsea Bay in December, the window of Driftwood Island would always have undergone a dramatic transformation. It was still filled with beautiful hand-made items, but they were all Christmas themed. The first year they'd visited, Colleen had bought a string of tiny wooden, red and white striped candy canes, which she'd threaded around the middle of the Christmas tree every year up until the year she'd died. They were what Freya had been so desperate to find, and take to the new flat in London, when she'd come across the journal.

'Come on girl, let's go and see if they've got something special in this year.' Ginger trotted along behind her, as they passed the delicatessen that Ellie had said her sister-in-law owned. The smell of ginger and cinnamon drifted out onto the street as she passed, and a choir was singing Christmas carols outside the chapel that was almost opposite Drift-wood Island, collecting money for charity in a silver bucket with a strand of tinsel tied around it's middle. There was no denying that Christmas was creeping up behind her, but she'd never felt less festive in her life. Maybe she should have headed somewhere with no memories of Christmas past, or a place where they barely acknowledged the season of goodwill – somewhere with a single Christmas tree in the town square, instead of in almost every shop window like Kelsea Bay.

'What do you think about the stars?' Freya stopped outside the window of Driftwood Island, her eyes immediately fixing on the string of wooden stars, painted in a shabby chic style with antique gold. Auntie Linda would hate them, they were so under-stated, but her mother would have loved them, and she did too. 'I think they're the ones, don't you, Ginger? And Mum always loved this shop so much.' If talking to a dog was the first sign of madness, then she was well on her way.

'I don't know about her, but I think they're great.' The voice behind her made Freya jump and she knocked her shoulder against the window of Driftwood Island as she spun around. 'I'm so sorry, I didn't mean to frighten you.'

'It's fine.' Freya's cheeks burned, as Ellie's husband gave her an apologetic smile. She'd been introduced to Ben, when he'd dashed back to the farm to take Karen in to get her wrist checked out. They'd also insisted that she join them in the farmhouse for dinner that night, after Karen had been given the all-clear. She'd met Karen's husband, Alan, then too, and he was now standing alongside Ben and another man, who she didn't know. Having them all catch her talking to Ginger was embarrassing, but if they thought so too, none of them were showing it.

'Freya, this is Seth by the way.' Ben gestured towards the good-looking blond man standing between him and Alan. 'He's my best mate and he's engaged to Ellie's best friend, Liv. Or at least he's about to be!'

'You are the worst person ever at keeping a secret!' Seth shot Ben a look, and then laughed, turning towards Freya and holding out his hand. 'The three of us decided to go Christmas shopping together in the hope that a trio of clueless idiots were better than one! I spotted a diamond ring in Ruby Tuesdays, the jewellers at the top of the high street, and I just knew it would be perfect for Olivia. It's supposed to be the biggest secret since how someone with a belly Santa's size can squeeze down all those chimneys. But if blabbermouth here carries on the way he is, Liv will know about it before I even get home.'

'Congratulations and nice to meet you.' Freya returned his smile. 'But don't worry, I'm very good at keeping secrets. As you might have spotted, I only really talk to Ginger these days.'

'Animals are often better confidantes than people, in my experience.' Alan looked at her shyly. He'd been as welcoming to her as the rest of the family at Seabreeze Farm, but she could sense he felt a bit awkward around new people.

'I've got to say I'm inclined to agree.' Freya smiled again. Given how badly she'd been let down by some people just lately, Ginger definitely seemed a better option. But opening up to Ellie and Karen had helped, too. So maybe there were still some people she could learn to trust, she was just going to have to be a hell of a lot pickier in future. 'How did the rest of your Christmas shopping go?'

'There was a lot of panic buying involved.' Ben grinned and raised the shopping bags he was carrying, to prove the point. 'But my strategy involved buying as much stuff as possible, in the hope that at least one of the presents will be something she was hoping for.'

'All I want for Christmas is that baby of yours to be safely delivered. It's about the best present a man could wish for, anyway, to be a granddad.' Alan shrugged. 'I mean I know I'm not Ellie's real dad, but it doesn't make a jot of difference to me.'

'And it won't to the baby either.' Maybe Ben would have hugged his father-in-law, if he hadn't had his arms full of shopping, and if Alan had been a *hugging-in-public* sort of man. Freya barely knew him, but it was pretty obvious from the little bit of time she had spent with him that he definitely wasn't that sort of man.

'Do you want us to hold on to Ginger, while you go in and get the decoration you were looking at?' Seth gestured towards the window display and it took a second or two for Freya to register what he was saying. She'd forgotten all about the decoration, listening to Alan talk about Ellie's baby. Even if she met someone else, now that Ollie was out of her life, she wouldn't have that moment of joy – telling her parents that they were going to have a grandchild. If she'd still been with Ollie, his parents would have been thrilled, of course. And the same would probably go for any future in-laws she might have – if she ever managed to trust another man again. But it wouldn't be the same as having *her* mum and dad there, and the loss of them hit her all over again, like a blast of cold December air.

'Thank you, but I think I'll leave it until tomorrow, so I

can come back down when the shops aren't about to close up and have more of a look around before I decide.'

'Are you heading back to the farm now? We can give you a lift home if you are, I think we're all shopped out.' Ben stepped forward to let another shopper pass him on the pavement.

'Oh, no, don't worry, Ginger and I can walk back.'

'Not in this light you can't. There's not even a pavement on the road that leads back to the farm, and Karen and Ellie would never forgive us if something happened to you and you got hit by a car or something.' Alan suddenly sounded assertive and he clearly wouldn't be taking no for an answer. 'Not to mention the fact that I would never forgive myself.'

'Well I guess that settles it then.' Ben turned to Freya again. 'We're parked down there, just overlooking the bay.'

'Thank you, you've all been so kind.' Turning to head back down the hill, she blinked back the threatened tears for the hundredth time since the day she'd found the journal. It was hard not to envy Ellie, surrounded by people she loved, and about to add to that number by becoming a mum. Envy might be an ugly emotion, but Freya was only human after all.

* * *

'Are you sure we can't persuade you to join us for dinner again tonight, as a thank you for taking Ginger out? The last thing I feel like doing is going out walking these days.' Ellie looked down at the little dog, stretched out in front of the Aga. Having Freya around was turning out to be an unexpected bonus, and not just because of the dog walks. She'd said she wanted to keep busy on the day of the wedding, but she'd asked if she could carry on helping out until she left after Christmas. And Ellie couldn't deny how handy it was to have the extra pair of hands with Karen still laid up.

'I don't want to keep gate-crashing.' Freya smiled, but it didn't quite reach her eyes.

'You wouldn't be doing that and, I don't know what you've heard, but I promise I won't be the one doing the cooking!'

'It's not that. I'm just not sure I'll be great company tonight, but don't worry I won't be sitting around listening to the song that would have been our first dance.' Freya tried to laugh, but it sounded hollow, and she shook her head. 'I'm going to ring my aunt and have a long chat with her, before she heads off to Australia tomorrow. I want to see if she's been able to find out any more about who my dad might be.'

'Did she manage to send a copy of the photo to you?' Ellie had come up with the plan, when Freya had told them about her mother's journal and the photograph of the man she was certain was her father, that had been hidden between the pages. If they had the photo, and asked around in Kelsea Bay, there had to be someone who knew who the man in the picture was.

'I still can't believe I didn't pick it up before I left.' Freya shook her head again. 'But I was just so desperate to get away before Ollie came looking for me again. My uncle Dave said he'd scan the photo in, so he could email it to me, and I'm hoping he's been able to do that before he goes away.'

'If you change your mind about coming to eat with us, you only have to say the word.' Ellie didn't want to push Freya if she really wanted to be on her own, but she couldn't help hating the thought of it. It was bad enough that Christmas was less than two weeks away, but Freya spending what would have been her wedding night, all on her own, just didn't seem right. There was one little thing she could do to help, though. 'Even if you don't change your mind, do you think you could email me your bank details, so that I can pay some money into your account?'

'What money?'

'Your payment for the wedding venue hire.'

'But you can't do that! I cost you a booking, and I knew I'd have to pay in full, cancelling that late.'

'Much as I'm really sorry about the break-up with your fiancé...' Ellie paused, wondering if she was about to make things worse. 'If I'm truthful, I was dreading having to do the wedding without Mum, while I feel like an Easter egg on legs, and half my casual staff are already booked up with other Christmas events.'

'You'll be out of pocket, though. You must have had to cover wages for the staff who were going to work, and pay out for other stuff.'

'A couple of the team were just happy to get a Saturday off so close to Christmas, and most of the others were able to take on hours doing other casual bar and waitressing work elsewhere, through the same agency I use. You've paid the deposits for the entertainment and the flowers yourself, and all the drinks were on sale or return anyway. We'd arranged for outside caterers with Mum not up to organising it, but they were able to re-use everything except for the cake. The barn would just have been sitting there empty if we hadn't taken your booking, which we wouldn't have done if we'd known I'd be pregnant by then, or that Mum would have been off her feet. So it really isn't a problem.' Ellie paused again, weighing up what she was about to say next. But Freya needed a friend, someone entirely on her side, so she'd have to risk causing offence and say it anyway. 'You said you were using the money your mum left you to pay for most of the wedding, so we thought this money should go back into your account and not anywhere that Ollie might be able to get his hands on it. I'm sure your mum would have wanted you to use it for a deposit for somewhere to live, now that your plans have changed. I know my mum would.'

'I don't know what to say.' Freya managed a wobbly smile and this time it reached her eyes, along with the tears that had sprung up there.

'It was the least we could do after you rescued Mum when she had her fall, and with you being so helpful around the farm too.' Ellie returned her smile. 'Although when I saw you being chased across the yard by Gerald and Dolly on that first day, I didn't think you'd be that keen to get involved with the animals.'

'I think they just took me by surprise, when I was already feeling a bit vulnerable! But I used to dream about working at your great aunt's donkey sanctuary, when I was a kid, so at least one of my dreams has come true.'

'Lots more of them will, I promise. If you're up to helping me out tomorrow, I can bore you with the details of how we came to take over the farm, and how close I came to marrying the wrong man before I met Ben. I might even tell you about the time that Gerald and Dolly wreaked havoc in the marquee, on the morning of our first ever wedding. It nearly ended up finishing the business before we'd even got to the end of day one!'

'I'd like that, if you're sure I'm not in the way.'

'Far from it.' Ellie reached out and squeezed her new friend's hand. Freya might have dropped into their lives unexpectedly, but it already felt like they'd been friends for a long time.

'If there's anything else I can do, just say, won't you?' Freya met her gaze. 'It comes to something when the kindness of people I've only just met, outstrips everything else. I still can't believe you're doing it and I can't thank you enough. But you're right, Mum would have wanted me to use the money to make sure I can start afresh.'

'That's settled then. And if you really do want to do even more to help than you already are, then spending a bit of time with Mum would be brilliant.' Ellie sighed. 'She's trying to be good, after nearly breaking her wrist, but I know sitting around doing nothing is slowly driving her out of her mind. I'd love to spend all day sitting with her, and chatting, but there's still so much going on with the last two Christmas events we've got coming up. If you could make time to have a cup of tea with her, once or twice a day, I'd feel far less guilty about leaving her to her own devices most of the time. She hates daytime TV at the best of times, but I think she's in danger of throwing the remote through the screen, if she has to sit through one more episode of *Loose Women*.'

'I'd love to do that, your mum's great. And you've all been so good to me.'

'Mum's a pretty big fan of yours too. In fact everyone is since you got her off the floor and sorted her wrist out, before she did any more damage to it.' Ellie looked down at Ginger again, who'd got to her feet. 'And this little lady seems to have completely fallen in love with you. Are you sure you don't mind her spending all her time with you and making herself at home on your bed in The Old Stables?'

'I've fallen in love with her too. So, if you're sure you don't mind, I'm more than happy for her to stay over there with me.'

'Of course, and there's only one condition.'

'Okay.' Freya narrowed her eyes, no doubt bracing herself for another request for help.

'Promise me you'll join us for dinner on Christmas Day?' Ellie waited for Freya to make an excuse, but this time she didn't.

'I'd really like that.'

'So would I.' Ellie's shoulders relaxed at last. Hopefully, by Christmas Day, they'd have the perfect present for Freya too – and she'd finally know who her biological father was.

7

Freya rested the cup of tea on the table in front of her and picked up her phone, accidentally catching sight of the time. Eight o'clock would have been roughly the time that the wedding breakfast was reaching a close, and the speeches were being toasted with champagne. Tea would have to do instead, when what she really needed was something that would knock her out until the day was finally over. If she was going to battle on through the rest of the day, she needed to see a familiar face, so Freya selected to FaceTime Auntie Linda, rather than just calling her.

'Oh lovey, you always do this when I'm looking like I've been chased through a hedgerow by a herd of wildebeest!' Auntie Linda attempted to angle the phone to hide the Sainsbury's carrier bag she was wearing on top of her head.

'Don't worry, I know all about your hair dyeing habits, and I'm sure you're going to look lovely when it's done.'

'Hmm.' Auntie Linda pursed her lips. 'Well the box promised to cover *every* grey hair, but it'll have its work cut out and at four ninety-nine a pack, I might be expecting too much of it. You look better than I thought you would, though.'

'I'm holding it together.' Ginger jumped on to the sofa and curled up against her leg. 'Coming down here to stay with Karen was the best thing I could have done.'

'I'm so pleased she's there for you, otherwise I really would have thought about cancelling the trip to see Scotty.'

'I know you would, but there's really no need. I've messed other people's plans up enough as it is, cancelling the wedding with so little notice.' Freya clenched her fist, the nails digging into her palm. There were wedding guests who she knew had booked hotel rooms, because they'd planned to travel up from Bristol, or other areas of the country. She just hoped they'd all had time to cancel them without incurring the full cost of the overnight stay. Guilt was already gnawing at her stomach, without working out what she'd cost her family and friends financially. Going through with the wedding would have been worse in the long run, though. She might even have had a child with Ollie, before she discovered how easy he found it to lie, and the repercussions of that could have gone on for years.

'Don't be silly, everyone who loves you understands, and they just want the best for you. I can't tell you how many people have called me to see how you are.'

'They're probably just being nosey.'

'Not all of them.' Auntie Linda wrinkled her nose, making the Sainsbury's bag slide down her forehead until she pushed it back up again. 'Ollie turns up here every day; he even came this morning, begging me to give him your number before it was *too late*.'

'You don't think he'd do anything stupid do you?' Nausea swirled in her stomach; he might not have turned out to be the person she thought he was, but that didn't mean she could just turn off every feeling she had for him.

'No, I'm pretty sure that's not what he meant.'

'What do you think he meant, then?' Freya stared at the screen, but Auntie Linda was looking down.

'Oh, I don't know.' Her aunt was definitely avoiding eye contact, but she'd never been able to hide what she was thinking. The moment Freya had mentioned the possibility of John not being her birth father, she'd known she was right by the twitch at the corner of her aunt's eye. It had been the same when she'd confided that she thought Ollie might propose. Linda had tried to master the nonchalant air of someone not in the know, but it had been blatantly obvious from the look on her face that Freya had rumbled Ollie's plans. He'd proposed a week later, and she'd tried just as hard as her aunt to look surprised. Luckily she was far better at pulling it off. But when Ollie had told her that he'd asked her Auntie Linda and Uncle Dave for their approval in advance, she'd had to feign surprise all over again.

'You do know. Just tell me; it doesn't matter now anyway. It could hardly be any worse than what's already happened.' Thinking about it made Freya's stomach ache, but she wasn't going to admit to her aunt quite how much she was struggling.

'Okay, if you really want to know, he said if he hadn't heard from you by the time you would have been married, that he'd accept you meant it when you said it was over, and you wouldn't hear from him again. I did the right thing by not giving him your number, though, didn't I?'

'You did.' Freya's insides twisted over again, despite her certainty. She could hardly get her head around the prospect of never seeing Ollie again, but sometimes doing the right thing wasn't always easy.

'Sophie's been here, too.' Auntie Linda pursed her lips again. 'She said you've blocked her email address and obviously your old phone doesn't work any more. She asked if she could send me an email to forward to you.'

'I'm not interested.'

'She wants to explain what happened with Ollie. She told me some of it and, if what she said is true, I think you should hear him out because it really might not be what you think.'

'What's the point? Neither of them told me the truth when it really mattered, so how can I trust anything she says? He probably just put her up to it, to stop him looking like the bad guy.'

'Do you really believe Ollie could have fooled us all to that extent?' Linda's poker face was failing her again. She clearly didn't think so.

'It doesn't matter. He said it himself, it's too late now anyway. So what's the point of reading what Sophie has to say? She's just trying to offload her guilt on to me.'

'Okay, lovey, I'm sorry. Forget I mentioned it.'

'Did Uncle Dave manage to scan in those pictures?' Searching for her father was something Freya could focus on, a possibility of a future to look forward to, instead of the regret that swelled in her chest every time she thought about Ollie.

'Yes, he has. I was going to email them over after I've

rinsed this stuff off my hair.' Auntie Linda smiled. 'And we've got a bit more news for you, too.'

'Go on.' The ache in her stomach had been replaced by a fluttering in her chest. If her aunt and uncle had discovered something that could take her a step closer to finding her dad, then there might still be cause to bring out the champagne today after all.

'He's finally heard back from Denise.' Linda smiled again. 'She said she got his message on the day he sent it, but she was so shocked to hear from someone close to Colleen, that she had to think about it for a couple of days before replying.'

'But she was Mum's best friend, wasn't she?'

'Back then, she was. But when she spoke to Dave, she told him how hurt she was that your mother cut all contact with her when she got together with John. I think doing that was all part of your mum and dad's plan to keep their new lives separate from what had gone on before, but you can see how it would have upset her best friend, can't you?'

'Absolutely.' Freya didn't want to use up any more of her energy thinking about Sophie, but she knew only too well how much the actions of a so-called friend could hurt. 'I suppose they thought the fewer people around who knew the truth about my parentage, the less chance there was of me finding out.'

'I think you're right.' Linda sighed again. 'But once she heard what had happened, she was really sorry she hadn't had the chance to see your mum again before she died, and she offered to help as much as she could with tracking down your dad. I'm going to email the photos to her too, so she can ask around to see if any of the old crowd from the holiday camp know where he is now.'

'But she must know his name?' Freya didn't want to admit to her aunt that she'd already been in touch with some of her mother's other old friends, because based upon Denise's reaction it might not have helped. It was too late now though and she had to hope more than ever that Denise would come through.

'That's the tricky bit. She says she never knew his surname, but she thinks he was called Colin, because she remembers it being like a male version of your mum's name. Apparently Colleen hated that, and said it made them sound stupid. She was so image conscious back then.' Linda shrugged, but Freya still found that version of her mother almost impossible to reconcile with the woman she'd loved. There'd been so much she hadn't known about her mother, though. 'Anyway, to get around it, the Yellow Coats all gave your dad a nickname and called him Giles.'

'Why Giles?'

'Because he was a farmer. You know, like Farmer Giles from the Tolkien story?'

'Not really.' The fact that Auntie Linda knew who Tolkien was, came as a shock in itself – her reading material of choice was usually more along the lines of Danielle Steele.

'To be honest I didn't either, but your uncle Dave explained it to me. Can't stand all that bloody *Lord of the Rings* business myself, but Dave can't get enough of hobbits. I suppose that might explain why he's stayed with me so long!'

'He knows he got lucky when you married him.' Freya

laughed properly for the first time that day and blew her auntie a kiss. 'Did Denise remember anything else?'

'She admitted she'd chucked out a lot of stuff from when she was friends with your mum, including the photos she had of her during that last summer. Like I said, she was pretty upset about your mum cutting her off, so she didn't want too many reminders around. She's going to have a look through her things, though, just in case there's anything else. But I think our best hope is that one of the other people she talks to, from when your mum worked in the holiday park, might remember what Giles's real name was. I think sending the photo on to her, so she can put some feelers out, is a big step forward, lovey. I really do.'

'So do I.' Freya just hoped that her own messages hadn't already muddied the waters, especially if one of the people she contacted was still close to 'Giles', or Colin, or whatever the hell her father's name was. 'Thank you, and can you thank Uncle Dave for me too, please?'

'Of course I will, but there's no need to thank us, you're the closest thing we've got to a daughter and, as far as he's concerned, nothing's too much trouble for you. And I feel exactly the same.'

'You might not say that if I keep you talking any longer and all your hair falls out.' Freya laughed again at the expression that crossed her aunt's face.

'Oh God, you're right. I'll have to go, but I'll email you later, okay? And I'll FaceTime you when we get to Scotty's place. They'll all want to talk to you on Christmas Day, too.'

'Okay, give everyone my love in the meantime. Safe journey.' Freya pressed the button to end the video call, and offered up another Christmas wish. If the first was to find her birth father, then the second was even more important. She might only have a handful of people left who she could call family, but they'd all be in Australia for Christmas, and she needed them to stay safe. Otherwise she really would be all alone in the world, and not just for Christmas.

* * *

If someone told Freya she'd have to live in The Old Stables for the rest of her life it wouldn't have bothered her. Ellie really had thought of everything when she'd had the stables converted, including a state-of-the-art coffee machine and satellite television. If there was any way to convince herself that Christmas could still come right, after everything that had happened, it was the stream of feel-good movies on one of the satellite channels. No matter the odds, and how close to Christmas the characters' lives fell apart, it all came good in time for the twenty-fifth of December. Sadly, real life wasn't like a Hallmark movie, and good things didn't happen just because you wished for them. She couldn't do anything about making sure Auntie Linda and Uncle Dave got to Australia and back safely, but she could set about making her only other wish come true.

With another feel-good movie playing in the background, and Ginger snoring softly beside her, Freya switched on her laptop and opened the email from her aunt, clicking on the photos to download them without even reading the email. Uncle Dave had done a great job. Not only had he scanned in the photograph, but he'd added an enlarged version of just the man her mum had been hugging in the original picture. Staring at the image, Freya took in his features, trying to find a likeness. Did he have the same small kink in the cartilage of his ear as she did? The one that her mum had always assured her was barely noticeable. Maybe their similarities would turn out to be something less physical, like the way they laughed, or the fact she couldn't eat strawberries without coming out in a rash.

Saving the photographs, Freya scrolled up to the top of the email to see whether her aunt had anything else to say.

✉ Email from linda.keaveney@digiterweb.com

Dear Freya,

I hope the pictures are okay. Uncle Dave thought you might want one of just Colin, in case you want to ask around without giving the game away that it's linked to your mum. We really hope you find him, but I know part of the reason your mum never told you was because she knew you would want to find him, and she was scared you'd feel rejected if he didn't want a relationship. We're praying that won't be the case, but we don't want you hurt again either. Like I said when you first found out, you need to keep in mind that it might not end the way you want, even if you do find him.

Don't be cross, but I've forwarded on the email that Sophie sent me below. If you don't want to read it, that's fine, but I wanted to give you the chance to change your mind before we left for Australia.

Love you millions,

Auntie Linda xx

Freya looked up at the TV; a woman with perfect hair was laughing as she iced Christmas cookies with the object of her affection looking on, in front of a backdrop of twinkly

fairy lights, as the film reached its inevitably happy conclusion. But Auntie Linda was right, there was no guarantee of a
happy ending, and every chance that the search for her
father could just end up piling on another layer of
heartache. Maybe it would be easier to forget the idea altogether, and be thankful that John had come into her life
when he had and taught her that good men did exist. He'd
done a good enough job for her to hold on to that belief,
despite how things had turned out with Ollie. It was why she
could believe that Ellie's husband, Ben, would turn out to be
a great dad. And that his friend, Seth, would keep the
promises he made, when he presented his girlfriend with
the ring he'd just had to buy, whilst he was out Christmas
shopping. Despite her worries, coming to Seabreeze Farm
had proved she still had enough belief to trust in people
until they proved her wrong, and surely she owed her birth
father the same chance? If all he was prepared to do was
answer a few questions before he walked back out of her life,
that was fine. It would hurt, but it would be enough. She was
almost sure of that now.

Sophie wasn't owed a second chance, though, and a big
part of Freya wanted to slam down the laptop lid and ignore
the email that Linda had forwarded on. Keeping her eyes
fixed on the TV as the couple on screen stepped out onto the
streets of New York, with a snowstorm swirling around
them, Freya weighed up her options. She could ignore the
email and spend all night lying awake wondering what it
said, before giving up at 3 a.m. and finally reading it. Or she
could delete it and give herself no choice but to forget the
whole thing. Then there was the third option, just to read
the goddamn thing. In the end, curiosity got the better of

her; exactly as it had with the note Ollie had sent with the locket.

✉ Forwarded email from: sophiechaletgirl1992@ mallowmail.com

Hi Freya,

If you're reading this, thank you. I know what it must have looked like when you saw me and Ollie together and you're not wrong about me. I realised a while back that I had feelings for him. I always have, I guess, but I didn't want to admit it. I know it was wrong to tell him, but I couldn't let the chance pass by without letting him know how I felt, just in case he felt the same. Only he didn't, and he wanted to tell you and get it all out in the open, but I just couldn't give up. I convinced myself that if I kept meeting with him, he'd finally see it too. When he said he wouldn't meet me again, I told him I wouldn't be able to handle it if he didn't. I'm ashamed to admit it, but I said I couldn't see the point of living if he married you. I thought I meant it, too, until I saw your face when you walked into the restaurant and, worse than that, the look on his face. He's never looked at me like that, no one has, and I knew then and there that he never would. He made a mistake not telling you what I was doing, but his intentions were all good. He didn't want to risk me hurting myself, and he didn't want to hurt you unnecessarily by having you find out what an awful friend I was. I don't expect you to forgive me, but if this helps you to forgive Ollie, then I might at least be able to start forgiving myself.

Sophie xx

The first time Freya read it, she barely took in a word. Her internal dialogue, about not listening to anything either of them said, was shouting far too loud. By attempt number three she'd got the gist of it, but she was no nearer to deciding how much of it was true. It still didn't justify why Ollie hadn't told her what was going on; they were supposed to be able to tell each other everything. Sophie's version of events could easily have been something the two of them had cooked up between them. It didn't change anything. Freya slid her fingers across the mouse pad, hovering over the icon for the wastepaper bin, but for some reason she couldn't bring herself to delete the message. She could have convinced herself it was because she didn't want to delete Auntie Linda's email with it – but she'd already checked that the downloaded photos had saved, and she wasn't going to start lying to herself. It was bad enough that everyone else seemed determined to lie to her, without going down that path.

'What do you think?' Ellie twirled around, grinning at Karen and Freya, as she flicked the switch to turn on the Christmas lights.

'It's perfect.' Karen couldn't help smiling in response. Ellie might be at the stage where she was struggling to put on her socks, but she'd done a grand job of dressing the Christmas tree that Alan had insisted on putting in the sitting room, so that Karen would have something pretty to look at while she continued the tedious process of recovery. It already felt as though she'd had her leg in plaster since the Christmas before, and boredom didn't even come close to describing her frustration. The girls had tried to make it easier for her, though. Ellie spent as much time with her as she could, and having Freya around had really helped too. Then there was Liv, Ellie's best friend. Now that she'd finished teaching for the Christmas holidays, she was helping out on the farm too, freeing up more of Ellie's time, and popping in for a chat when she could. It was funny, Karen had always dreamt of having a house full of kids, but for a number of reasons she'd ended up only having Ellie, and although she counted her lucky stars, every day, that she had her daughter, it was nice to have all three of them popping in and out to spend time with her, and they'd all miss Freya when she left after Christmas.

'Was yours the coffee, Karen?' Liv came into the room with a tray of drinks and a plate of shop bought shortbread biscuits. Karen couldn't help wishing she'd been able to make them. She'd missed baking too, far more than she'd ever have thought she would.

'Yes, that's me. Thanks sweetheart.' Karen took the mug from Liv. At least she could manage that, even with a sprained wrist.

'What do you think of the garlands of stars, Mum?' Ellie adjusted one of the loops in the string of wooden stars that she'd wrapped around the tree.

'They're beautiful; where did you get them?'

'Driftwood Island,' Ellie and Freya answered at the same time.

'Sorry.' Freya held up a hand. 'It's just that I spotted them in the window, too, a couple of days ago, and I thought they'd go perfectly with the other decorations that Mum bought from Driftwood Island over the years. I was going to go back into town later this week and pick some up.'

'I bought too many strands, if you want one of ours?' Ellie took a cup from Liv as she spoke.

'I couldn't possibly take anything else from you.' Freya shook her head.

'Yes you can, I'll drop them over to The Old Stables later so you can put them on your tree in there, then you can take them home when you go.' Ellie turned back to the tree, before Freya could offer any further argument.

'I wanted to ask you to do me another favour, actually.' Freya ran a finger around the rim of her cup. 'My aunt emailed over the photo of my birth father, the one that I found in Mum's journal, and I wondered whether you might be able to print a few copies out and ask around, in case it jogs anyone's memory? It might make people a bit more willing to talk, because they know you. If I just turn up out of the blue and start asking around, they might wonder if I've got some ulterior motive.'

'Of course we will.' Karen didn't have to wait for Ellie to respond, she already knew how much her daughter wanted to help their new friend.

'I can go and get on with something else outside if you guys want to talk?' Liv was already backing out of the room when Freya shook her head.

'No, please don't. It would help me out if as many people can ask as possible.' Freya smiled at her. 'How much do you know about why I'm here?'

'Nothing, other than that you called off your wedding.' Liv sat down closest to Karen, as Freya nodded her head.

'I did, but the reason we booked Seabreeze Farm in the first place is because Mum loved Kelsea Bay, and she'd bring me up here to see the animals every year, when it was still a donkey sanctuary. I always knew it was close to her heart, but I never knew the real reason why, until I found a journal of hers and some old photos, when I was packing up mine and Ollie's flat to move house. That's when I discovered that the man I'd always thought was my dad, wasn't my biological father. And that Mum had fallen pregnant with me whilst she was down here doing a summer season, as an entertainer at one of the local holiday parks.'

'That must have been such a shock.' Liv was clearly struggling to know what to say, but what *could* you say to someone who'd made as startling a discovery as Freya had, having spent almost thirty years believing in something that wasn't true?

'I was angry with Mum at first, but the more I've talked it through with my aunt, and Karen' – Freya turned to her and smiled – 'the more I know she was only doing it to protect me.'

'So you don't know anything about this man?' Liv raised her eyebrows, as Freya shook her head.

'My uncle tracked down an old friend of Mum's, and she thinks his name was Colin, but even that's not a definite. One thing I do know is that he was a farmer, and they all used to call him Giles as a nickname.'

'If he was a farmer, then he's more likely to have been a local, rather than a holiday maker just passing through.' Ellie tapped her teeth with the pen she'd picked up from the Welsh dresser. 'We need to write some of these things down, so that we have as much information as possible when we ask around. I'm really sorry, but I've forgotten what you said your mum's name was.'

'It was Colleen, but I don't want to mention her, at least

not at first.' Freya breathed out. 'I want to see if I can track my father down. And given that he wasn't interested in having anything to do with me when Mum was pregnant, I don't want to give him the opportunity to do a runner before I've even had a chance to catch a glimpse of him. That's assuming he's still alive.'

'Oh God, I hadn't thought of that.' Karen shook her head. No one could have that much bad luck, surely?

'Let's not worry about that for now.' Ellie rested her mug on the top of her bump. 'The first priority is to get some copies of the photo printed and start asking around. There must be someone around here who recognises him. I think it's really exciting.'

'It will be if we find him.' Freya bit her lip, and, if Karen could have got up, she'd have gone over and hugged her. But all she could do was metaphorically cross her fingers and hope for the best.

8

Freya shivered as the sea breeze hit her full in the face. It was a week until Christmas, and the temperature was dropping on a daily basis. Ginger didn't seem to feel the cold, though, and was rushing through the foamy surf as if it was a summer's day.

Ellie and Liv had been true to their word and had spoken to as many local people as possible to try and track down her father, but there'd only been a handful of red herrings and no solid leads so far. Freya had paid their efforts back by helping out at the last big corporate event of the year – the Christmas party for a large agricultural insurance company, which Ellie had told her provided a good chunk of the farm's income. Working alongside Ellie and Liv had been good fun, like being back on the ward again. It was strange to think that, in just a few weeks, she'd be starting her new job, as a senior sister on the cardiac ward of a London hospital. She might not be going ahead with her plan to share a life with Ollie in the capital, or be moving to the flat they'd been so excited to find, but she'd still be starting her new job. There was no choice, at least not in the short term, and she'd have to start looking for somewhere to live as soon as Christmas was over.

Renting a flat in central London by herself wasn't an option, so she'd have to look for something in a neighbouring county, which was a commutable distance from the hospital. She couldn't face the thought of flat sharing and, in truth, she didn't want to think too much about leaving The Old Stables. Maybe she could find somewhere to rent nearby, or at least elsewhere in Kent. Kelsea Bay felt as close to somewhere she could call home, as anywhere had since she'd sold her parents' house, just after her mother had died.

Turning to head back to the well-worn stone steps that led up from the stretch of beach she and Ginger chose to walk on most days, the wind whipped at Freya's hair, blowing it across her face. When she pushed it out of her eyes, and turned back to make sure Ginger was following her, the little dog had disappeared.

'Ginger!' Scanning the shoreline, she could just make out the outline of the dog chasing after her favourite prey – a seagull. 'Come on Ginger, stop, please!' Freya shouted, and for a second she thought the dog might actually respond to the command. Ginger stopped and looked back to where Freya was standing. Then the seagull swooped past her again, sending her into a frenzy of barks as she skidded across the sand after the bird. Seconds later, Freya had lost sight of her all together.

'Oh God, please don't drown.' She started running in the direction that Ginger had gone, but as she got closer to the shoreline, her progress slowed down as her feet began to sink deeper and deeper into the wet sand. It was like running through wet concrete, and there was still no sign of Ginger. Ellie had trusted Freya to take care of the dog, and Ginger had been a lifesaver since she'd got to the farm. She'd listened without judging, and she hadn't even seemed to mind when Freya had soaked her fur with tears, on the morning after what should have been her wedding day when the sense of relief she'd expected had failed to arrive. If something happened to the dog, it would be the final straw.

Half an hour later, Freya was hotter than she'd ever dreamt she could be on a cold winter's day. It felt like she'd done a marathon, and her chest was tight with the effort of running and calling after the dog, but there was still no sign of her. Tears were streaming down her face and she didn't have a clue what to do. Were you supposed to report a missing dog to the RSPCA, or the police? She should probably ring Ellie first, but she couldn't bring herself to admit what she'd done, not until she really had to.

As she turned back towards the stone steps for what seemed like the hundredth time, there was a screech of brakes and a car honking its horn, up on the coast road. Breaking into a run, despite her legs feeling like they'd turned to jelly, Freya started to pray again. If Ginger had been knocked down, then the best thing she could do was to keep running and stop dragging Ellie, and the rest of her family, into the mire of bad luck that seemed to follow Freya around wherever she went.

'Hey, watch it!' She'd turned a hard right at the top of the stone steps, to head up to the coast road, and gone slap bang into a man who'd been heading in the other direction.

'Alan.' Freya tried to hold onto her composure as she registered who it was, but as soon as he realised it was her, and switched his expression from a scowl to a smile, she dissolved into noisy sobs. The poor man took at least two steps back, before he reached out and took hold of her shoulders.

'What's the matter, my love? I can't help you until I know what's wrong, but whatever it is, it can't be as bad as all that.'

'I've l-l-lost Ginger and there's a good chance she's just been knocked down by a car.' Half of Freya wanted to run up to the road to find out, but the other half didn't want to know how bad it really was and she wasn't sure she could remember how to move.

'I thought this was about your... *wedding*.' He pronounced the word slowly, as he dropped his hands back to his side. 'But a lost dog I can cope with and we've had more than our fair share of runaway animals at Seabreeze Farm. Don't worry, I'm sure we'll be able to find Ginger together, she'll just be chasing after a bird again, if I know her. What makes you think she's got on to the road?'

'I heard a car honking its horn and braking sharply just now. She's definitely not on the beach any more, so she must have headed that way.'

'I'll go up and check, just sit here for a moment and I'll come back if there's no sign of her on the coast road.' Alan was reassuringly calm as he guided her to a bench that looked out over the bay, and she didn't offer any argument. She should have been the one to go and check whether Ginger had run out into the road, but she couldn't face it.

Crossing her fingers, as Alan disappeared up to the road, she held her breath, listening out for the sound of him shouting that the dog had been knocked over and it was all her fault. Not that she needed anyone to tell her that. She'd let the shockwaves of discovering the truth about her father impair her judgement again and this time the consequences might be fatal.

'Well she's not up there.' Alan was puffing as he got back down to the bench, and Freya turned her tear-stained face towards him.

'Do you think there's a chance she could have run all the way home?' She crossed her fingers again, but it was too much to hope that the little dog was already back at the farm, curled up on the rug in front of the farmhouse's wood burning stove where she belonged.

'I suppose there's a chance, but Ginger has always been one to stick close to Ellie or Karen, unless a bird flies past and then no amount of yelling her name makes a blind bit of difference. Don't worry my love, she's a hardy little thing and she's street wise for a country dog, so I'm sure she'll turn up right as rain.' Alan's kindness was incredible, given the fact that she'd lost his family's beloved pet.

'She probably just had enough of me. Everyone I love leaves me in the end.' She hadn't meant for that last part to come out, and poor old Alan obviously had no idea what to say in response. He put a hand on her shoulder instead.

'I know one place where she could be, down by White-Cliff Cave. There are a lot of birds that roost there, and up on the cliff face above it, even in the winter. It'll be Ginger's idea of heaven, trying to get hold of one. Not that she'll ever do it;

I've seen stuffed toys with more hunting skills than that silly old dog.'

'Where's White-Cliff Cave?'

'It's on the far side of the bay. It'll be quicker if we walk along the coast road and down the steps at that end, instead of going across the beach, especially at the rate the tide is coming in.' Alan gestured towards the road with his head. 'The quicker we get moving, the quicker we can track her down and get you home in front of the fire. You look cold to the bone.'

'I was boiling hot from running across the beach to look for Ginger, but as soon as I sat down, all the warmth seemed to drain out of me again.' Freya stood up. 'But I don't care if I have to wade through icy water, as long as we find Ginger.'

'If we can beat the tide, we should be able to check out the cave and track down the little tinker without even getting our feet wet, but we best get moving. You just need to follow me.'

For a big man, Alan could move pretty quickly, and Freya had to step out to keep up with him, but she'd happily have run all the way there if she knew where White-Cliff Cave was. She just hoped he was right, because if the little dog wasn't there, they'd have to head back up to the farm and report her missing. There was no chance of having a conversation with Alan at the pace they were moving, and she wondered if that was part of the reason why he was walking so fast. She got the feeling that conversations weren't his strong point, at least not with a virtual stranger like her, but she was glad he was there. And not just because she wouldn't have had any idea about White-Cliff Cave if he hadn't been.

'We need to take these steps, just watch your footing. Not many people use this end of the beach, especially at this time of year, and there's probably still a tonne of seaweed you'll have to make your way over, that's been washed up from the last storm.'

'Thanks for the heads up.' Freya picked her way carefully down the steps. Alan hadn't been exaggerating when he'd mentioned the seaweed, but there were lumps of driftwood, too, as well as rocks and even a wrecked lobster pot, upended on the third step from the bottom.

'The cave is carved out of the cliff about a hundred feet to the left of here. We'll have to keep an eye out for the tide, though. If it comes in too far for us to get back to the steps, the only way up will be via the cliff face. And I don't know about you, but my days of being able to shin up a cliff face are long behind me.'

'I think the days of being able to shin up a cliff face bypassed me all together.' Freya managed a half-laugh. 'I never even managed to shin up a gym rope in my PE lessons at school.'

'We'd better get a move on then.'

Freya followed Alan along the narrow stretch of beach that led to the mouth of the cave. The walls of the cliff face around it were dripping with green algae, and the sound of so many birds was like something from a horror movie. It suddenly dawned on Freya that she barely knew the man she'd followed to a deserted patch of beach, where no one would hear her scream. The cave looked like the perfect place to dump a body too, and the seagulls would probably strip away the evidence before anyone even realised she was missing.

'Freya.' Alan put his hand on her arm again, as he said her name, and she almost leapt into the sea behind them.

'Oh my God, you made me jump!'

'It's all right, I think I can see her, up there to the left of the cave opening.' Alan pointed towards where he was looking and, sure enough, Ginger was creeping along a narrow ridge, towards where a group of gulls were sitting in a row.

'How the hell are we going to get her down?'

'We can try calling her, but I think our best bet is to let the seagulls do it for us.' Alan turned to look at her. 'They flock together for warmth and protection at this time of year, and the likelihood is that one of them will go for her before she has the chance to get much closer. If you've ever seen them nick a bag of chips off a kiddie down by the seafront, then you'll know they're more than capable of giving Ginger a flea in her ear.'

'What if she falls?'

'If she's scrambled up there okay, then she should be able to scramble down. I don't think it'll do us any favours to go up to her. She'd probably walk away from the whole thing whilst we were stuck up there, waiting for the air ambulance or the coastguard to come to our rescue.' Alan looked up at the cliff face again. 'I just hope the seagulls see her off before the tide comes all the way in.'

'Has she ever done this before?'

'She managed to climb up on the hay bales in one of the barns and squeeze through a gap in the corrugated iron, to get up on the roof. We had to borrow a cherry picker off Ben's friend, Julian, to get her down. She was after pigeons that time.'

'I thought it was cats that were meant to be obsessed with catching birds.' Ginger sounded like she had quite a history with feathered prey, but luckily for the birds it didn't sound like she had a lot of skill.

'She's always had a bit of an identity crisis our Ginger. We found her tied up in the caravan park next to my farm, after the family who owned her left her behind when they went home. Put it this way, I don't think she'd even been for a walk before we got her, never mind run after a ball. She's just making up for lost time and it's why we can't really get cross with her, even when she puts us through stuff like this.' Alan smiled and for the first time since Ginger had disappeared, some of the tension left Freya's spine. He might not be the most effusive of people, but he had a gentle warmth that was starting to make her believe that everything really could turn out okay.

'She's getting pretty close to that big gull on the edge of the flock now.' Freya could barely watch, suddenly wishing she could be quite as confident as Alan that the dog wasn't about to plunge to the ground from a great height.

'Watch him, he's sizing her up.' Alan shielded his eyes with his hand, as they looked up again, towards where the winter sun was slowly slipping down behind the cliff. 'He's going to go for her.'

The seagull looked at least twice the size of Ginger from where Freya was standing, but by the time it had opened its wings in a gesture of undisguised aggression, it looked more like four times her size. The little dog stood her ground for all of about two seconds, before trying to back along the narrow ledge. It was like watching a video on high-speed reverse, but her escape clearly wasn't happening fast enough for Ginger, as the bird continued to flap its wings and squawk at her. Deciding that turning around would be the quickest way out of there, Ginger lost her footing and Freya let out a gasp.

'It's okay, she's coming down on the diagonal. Never mind acting like a cat by chasing all those birds, I reckon our Ginger has got a touch of mountain goat in her blood.'

'I can't believe she's made it down in one piece.' Freya didn't know whether to laugh or burst into tears again, as the dog leapt off the bottom two feet of the cliff face and on to the sand, before trotting over to them, as casually as she might have done if she'd been let off the lead just two minutes before. Glancing at her watch, Freya could hardly believe she'd been looking for the dog for almost two hours. Although she felt about ten years older.

'We best get up on the coast path if we're going to make it home in one piece, too.' Alan clipped Ginger's lead onto her collar and Freya suspected it would be a long time before the dog sampled the freedom of an open beach again. She certainly wouldn't be letting her off for a run in a hurry. 'I'll give you both a lift back up to the farm, and we can tell Karen what this little tinker has been up to. It'll give her a laugh at least.'

'As long as it does someone some good, I suppose it can't be called a complete disaster.' Freya raised a questioning eyebrow, as Alan nodded in response – thoughts of John, the man who'd raised her as his own, suddenly popped into her head. She and Ellie might both have missed out on having birth fathers who wanted to be around, but it had made room for some pretty special men to come into their lives instead.

* * *

Karen held up the knitting and tried to stretch it square. It turned out that being good at cake-making didn't naturally translate into being good at other crafts. So far she'd tried crochet, knitting, scrap-booking and embroidery. The only thing she'd been able to complete was the adult colouring book that Ellie had bought for her, from the bookshop in town. Barely sixty, and resigned to a life where the biggest challenge she could overcome was keeping her colouring pens within the lines. Tempting as it was to try and stand as often as possible, she daren't risk it after almost breaking her wrist. Never mind the extra problems it would create, she wanted to be able to hold her first grandchild in her arms, when he or she arrived in January. So she had to behave herself, even if she did feel like hurling the knitting – needles and all – straight into the wood burning stove.

'Hello? Karen, are you in there?' Alan's deep voice seemed to bounce off the walls, as he called down the corridor.

'Where else would I be? At a Zumba class down in Kelsea Bay community centre?' Chance would be a fine thing, but the hospital had warned her there might be months of physio ahead before she could get back to normal. Not that Zumba was normal for her even when she wasn't laid up. Who needed an exercise class when you had a farm, a wedding venue, and a catering business to run?

'Sorry love, you know what I mean.' Alan gave her a sheepish grin as he came into the room, holding Ginger on a lead, with Freya just behind him.

'It's me who should be sorry. Being cooped up like this is

turning me into a proper old grump.' Karen felt better just for seeing them, and the knitting could definitely wait. 'What have you three been up to? Looks like it's windy out there.' Alan's hair was sticking up on end, which it was liable to do, seeing as he was almost religious in his rejection of hair products. They were for city boys with too much time on their hands, as far as he was concerned. But Freya was looking distinctly windswept too, and Ginger's coat was damp and curly, giving off that distinctive wet dog smell.

'Ginger decided to go seagull hunting up on the cliff face directly above White-Cliff Cave.' Alan unclipped the dog's lead, and she flopped down on the mat in front of the wood burner to dry off, clearly exhausted by her antics.

'You can tell me all about it over a cuppa, I'm gasping.' Karen pushed against the base of her chair to reposition herself, and to stop her buttocks from going completely numb. It was a losing battle. 'I'd like to say that not being able to make a pot of tea is the worst thing about being stuck like this, but it's not even close.'

'I can do it.' Freya was halfway out the door before Karen could even respond. 'And Alan can tell you all about Ginger's adventure whilst I'm gone. I'm not sure I can face re-living that one just yet.'

By the time Freya returned with the drinks, Karen had heard all about what Ginger had put her through, and Alan had confided that he'd found her in floods of tears on the path between the beach and the coast road. Ellie and Liv hadn't had much luck asking around about the photos so far, and Alan had been a bit reluctant to get involved in 'an episode of EastEnders', as he called it. But now he'd got to know Freya a bit better, Karen was sure he'd want to do his bit to help her out too. He could be prickly at first, her husband, but he had a heart of gold under all that bluff, and it hadn't taken her long to find it. He'd lived in Kelsea Bay all his life too, so if anyone could track down someone who might have known Freya's father, it would be him.

'Have you heard any more from your aunt, sweetheart?' Karen looked at Freya and her heart sank as the younger woman shook her head.

'I don't want to call her yet, to ask if they've heard more from mum's old friend, because she and Uncle Dave haven't seen my cousin Scotty and his family in over two years. I can't expect everyone to make it their priority, just because it was mine.' Freya swallowed so hard that Karen heard it.

'It was your priority? Have you changed your mind then?' Karen searched Freya's face, as Alan busied himself flicking through the Christmas edition of the *Radio Times*.

'I don't know, I've just got to thinking that maybe some things are best left alone. If my father didn't want to know about me back when mum was expecting me, what are the chances of him welcoming me into his life now?' Freya shook her head. 'One minute I'm determined to find him and it's the only thing I can think about, because I can't imagine a future where I never know who he is. Then the next minute I think about John, the man who brought me up. I couldn't have asked for a better dad, so why would I want to try and track down someone else who can never compare to him? I've spent hours on the internet searching through social media and every website that has any refer-ence to Kelsea Bay, but I haven't turned up anything yet. You guys have all been so brilliant asking around, but that's been a dead end too and I can't help wondering if the universe is trying to tell me something.'

'I know it seems impossible, but in my opinion there's every chance of him welcoming you into his life if he gets to know you.' For someone who was pretending not to be listening, Alan was lightning quick with his response.

'Alan's right, and you can't give up now, not when you've come so far.' Karen felt a prickle of guilt on the back of her neck. In all honesty, she couldn't be sure if her attempt to persuade Freya to keep searching was entirely based on looking out for the younger woman's welfare, or whether the excruciating boredom of being laid up was making her seek out whatever vicarious excitement she could get. There was almost certainly a dash of that somewhere in the mix, but Freya had been so desperate to find her father, so determined for at least one positive thing to come out of the discovery – and the subsequent ending of her engagement – that there had to be something they could all do to help.

'Let Alan take a look at the picture. If anyone will know a farmer from back then it's him.' She looked across at her husband, as he gave an almost imperceptible nod. 'He's not had time to get involved in much asking around yet, have you love? But the Christmas farmers' market in Elverham would be an ideal time for him to spread the word, even if he doesn't recognise your father from the picture.'

'This is the photo we're handing around.' Freya passed Alan the picture and he looked down at it. 'We're keeping Mum out of it for now, in case someone tells him who's looking for him and he puts two and two together and does a runner again before we even get the chance to speak.'

'Do you know him?' Karen's pulse seemed to quicken as

she waited for Alan to respond, so heaven knows how Freya was feeling.

'Can't say I do.' Even Alan looked disappointed. 'But that doesn't mean one of the other fellas down at the market won't know who he is. I was always the sort of bloke who kept myself to myself – socialising has never really been my sort of thing – so I wouldn't have got to know anyone down the pub or anything like that.'

'Have you got the version of the photo with your mum in, sweetheart? Just in case she and Alan ever bumped into each other in Kelsea Bay.'

'This is her, but she's got her head down, and curly blonde hair that's covering half of her face.'

'Ah the Kylie Minogue look! I didn't half fancy her back in the day.' Alan laughed as he looked at Karen. 'Sorry, love, I'm older and wiser now, and I know she's not a patch on you.'

'Hmmm. Well, with a body like mine, you're getting two Kylies for the price of one.'

'And I wouldn't swap you for a thousand Kylies. Trouble is, there was a time when everyone seemed to have a hair do like this, not just in Kelsea Bay either. I'm really sorry but neither of them ring any bells with me.' Alan handed the second photo back to Freya. 'But if you don't mind me keeping this one of your father, I'll definitely ask around at the farmers' market. Someone's got to know who he is, haven't they?'

'Of course they will.' Karen looked at Freya as she spoke, and prayed she was right. Something needed to happen to make the poor girl smile again, and if anyone deserved a bit of Christmas magic, it was Freya.

* * *

'You can stop looking at me like that, you don't deserve to be up on this sofa, let alone being fed treats.' Freya ran a hand over Ginger's coat, which had long since dried out from her seagull chasing adventure. 'Oh for God's sake, I've got about as much will-power as a wet lettuce leaf.' She walked across and took a dog chew out of the kitchen cupboard, turning around to give it to Ginger, who had shot off the sofa as soon as she heard the cupboard door open. Funny how she could hear that perfectly, but hadn't heard Freya desperately calling her name for well over an hour. The truth was she'd forgive the little dog anything because she'd fallen in love with her the first night Ginger had cuddled up next to her on the bed. She'd never really understood how devoted people were to their dogs until she'd met Seabreeze Farm's resident terrier. Ollie had always said that the first thing he wanted, when they could finally upsize from a flat and have their own garden, was a dog. He'd joked about it being good practice for when they had children, not to mention being the perfect companion for the kids as they grew up. He'd had it all planned out and his vision of their future had felt so real, but none of it had come to fruition and she knew she was grieving for a life she'd never had, as well as for the things they had shared.

'It's seven in the morning in Queensland; do you think that's too early to phone Auntie Linda, Ginger?' They were nine hours ahead of UK time, but although there was a risk of waking her aunt up by calling this early, at least it meant she'd catch her before they headed out for the day with Scotty and his family. 'Right, let's do it.'

Freya picked up her phone and selected the option of making a FaceTime call, hoping that it wouldn't stop her aunt from answering, if she was still in her PJs.

'Morning lovey! I was just about to call you, but we were trying to work out what the time difference was. I've been awake since 4 a.m. and I still don't know which way is up. This jet lag business is no joke and it seems to get worse the older I get.' Auntie Linda looked surprisingly bright-eyed, despite her claim that she'd barely slept. It obviously suited her being back with her grandchildren.

'I'm sorry to call so early, but I didn't want to interrupt you later.'

'You could never interrupt us, although your uncle Dave would have dragged me out of bed at 6 a.m. if I hadn't already been up, he's so excited. We're off to Brisbane today to do a tour of where they filmed one of the *Thor* movies. How have I got a husband in his mid-sixties, who's still so into films made from comic books stories? Honestly, the things I do for love!'

'Just tell me he's not wearing the costume he had for your last Halloween party?' Freya laughed as Linda pulled a face.

'It took some tough negotiation, I'm telling you. But I told him if he did that, I'd be wearing a teddy bear onesie. I think that just about swung it.'

'I'd love to see the reaction on the streets of Brisbane with you two dressed like that.' Freya suddenly wished she was with them and it had nothing to do with seeing them dress up to entertain the residents of Brisbane.

'We wish you were here too lovey.' Linda blew her a kiss. 'But thank goodness for the wonders of the internet, eh?'

'The Wi-Fi looks pretty good there. You're coming through loud and clear.'

'And you're coming through with all the subtlety of a brick!' It was Linda's turn to laugh. 'What you want to know, is whether we've heard anything else from Denise, right?'

'You got me.' Freya had to keep reminding herself that it probably wasn't going to be that easy, especially as every attempt to find out more about the mysterious Farmer Giles had been a road to nowhere so far. Even Alan, who'd lived in the area for over sixty years, didn't recognise him.

'We have heard from her, and I was getting to that, but I don't think you're going to be too pleased.' Linda's tone was suddenly serious, and heat flushed Freya's neck. This wasn't going to be good news.

'What is it?'

'The photo you've been asking around with – it's not your dad.' Linda's words hung in the virtual air between Australia and Seabreeze Farm for a few moments. As Freya struggled to undo all the images in her head, of meeting the man whose picture she'd stared at, at least ten times a day since she'd found it.

'I don't understand; how can it not be him?'

'Because it's not even your mum in the photo with him. Uncle Dave emailed it to Denise and she recognised it immediately, because it's her! She and your mum had matching hairstyles, but she remembered every detail of having the photo taken, and your mum was the one taking the picture. It was when Coll had gone down to see her, to tell her about the baby, and it turned out to be one of the last times she ever saw her, because Denise went off to work on a cruise ship not long after you were born, and then your mum broke off all contact.'

'If it's not my father, then who is the man in the picture?' Freya couldn't bring herself to let go of the hope, not until she was 100 per cent certain.

'She said it was her brother, Gary.'

'And she's sure he's not the one who, you know, was with Mum that summer? Maybe she's covering up for him, if he still doesn't want anything to do with me. I can't understand why Mum would have kept the photograph otherwise.'

'I thought the same, but Denise linked your uncle Dave and Gary up on Facebook, in case your mum had mentioned anything to him on that visit that she'd forgotten about.'

'And?' Freya held her breath.

'And your uncle Dave has got a new Facebook friend, but unfortunately that's about it. Gary backed up Denise's story, but he couldn't really offer anything else. Although Dave did find out something about Gary.'

'What?' There had to be something, because if Denise was another dead end she had absolutely no idea where to try and restart the search.

'That Gary has been married to a dentist called Nigel for the last five years, but they've been together since the mid-eighties. So unless Gary's taking his secret double life to extremes, then I'm afraid he's not your father.'

Tears stung the back of Freya's eyes; it was all starting to feel so hopeless. 'So where does that leave us, back at square one?'

'I hope not, lovey. Denise told Dave that she'd managed to unearth some more photos, not of your mum and dad, but some of the others who were around that summer, and she's sure a few of them were Kelsea Bay born and bred. There's bound to be someone there who recognises a face from the photos, and, if you can track them down, maybe it'll give us the clue we need.'

'Not exactly a solid lead though, is it?' Freya was determined not to cry, but she was struggling. She'd been so certain that she was keeping her expectations under control by constantly reminding herself that she might never find her father, or even if she did that he might reject her for a second time. She thought she'd come to terms with the prospect of giving up the search too, or maybe even choosing to, but now she knew that had been yet another lie.

'I'm sorry, lovey, but we won't give up.' Linda was giving this her all, but it wasn't her life and Freya couldn't allow it to consume her aunt, the way it was in danger of consuming her. The aftershocks of the discovery had already changed her life forever.

'I don't know; I think I need to set a time limit on it, because this isn't fair on you and there's a good chance I'll let the rest of my life slip away if I keep obsessing over this.' Freya didn't want to admit that part of her thought she already had, and she was determined not to ask if Linda had heard any more from Ollie. 'I've got a new job to start in January and I need to find somewhere to live before then. There are other things I've got to get on with. I can't spend all my time looking for a man who might be doing everything he can not to be found.'

'You could ring Ollie, and give him a chance to talk about what Sophie told you in that email... What?' Linda responded to the look that must have crossed Freya's face. 'I could hardly forward on her email without even reading it, could I?'

'I suppose not, but it doesn't matter anyway. Ollie made it clear that the wedding day was the cut-off point – it's too late, even if I did believe a word of Sophie's email.'

'It's never too late, unless you let it be.' Auntie Linda put her head on one side. 'If you tell him what happened on the morning before everything fell apart between you, I'm sure he'll understand. None of us can believe he'd deliberately do anything to hurt you and your mum always used to get misty eyed talking about the way he looked at you, because it reminded her so much of how John always looked at her. That's not something you should throw away without being absolutely certain that's it's broken.'

Freya couldn't speak for a moment; the way her mother had felt about Ollie was something that played on her mind in the darkness of the night. She'd completely adored him and had told Freya how much comfort it gave her to know she'd have Ollie once Colleen was no longer there. Except now she didn't, and even if she let someone into her life again one day, they'd never have known Colleen and another link to her beloved mother would be lost forever. She wished it was as easy as picking up the phone to Ollie and rewinding things to before it all went wrong, to unsay the things she'd said and to undo the lies he'd told her, for whatever reason he'd chosen to tell them. But life wasn't that simple and when Freya finally found her voice, it wasn't to respond to what her aunt had said.

'Say thanks to Uncle Dave for me, won't you?' She blew Linda a kiss. 'And give everyone my love. I'll call you again at about 8 a.m. your time on Christmas Day, if that's okay?'

'You can call me any time, lovey, you know that. But I'll email you again, when Denise sends the photos through, and keep your chin up in the meantime.'

'I will. Bye.' Freya ended the call and immediately broke her promise to her aunt, as her head dropped to her chest. The man in the photo wasn't her father, he was happily married to a dentist called Nigel, which meant she was further than ever from finding out who her real dad was. And the one person she wanted to pour her heart out to, who might have been able to make it all somehow more bearable, was no longer a part of her life. Some Christmas this was turning out to be.

9

'I know you've probably tried this already, but have you thought about registering your DNA on one of those websites, in case there's a match?' Ellie gave Freya a hopeful smile, as they did the morning round to feed all the animals. 'I read an article about twins who were separated for adoption just after they born and then found each other on one of those sites as adults. It's got to be worth a try?'

'I did it last year, after I lost Mum. Not asking her more about Dad... well, John's side of the family was one of my regrets. He was an only child and his parents died before he even met Mum. I realised how little I knew about his side after Mum died and Ollie being Ollie went straight out and got me one of those kits that can trace your ancestry, just so I'd know a little bit more.'

'Did it link you to anyone?'

'There were some very distant cousins in Canada, you know the third cousin, twice removed sort, but they turned out to be on Mum and Auntie Linda's side.' Freya sighed. It was starting to feel like half of her DNA had been created from a lab experiment because there didn't seem to be any trace of it anywhere.

'Are you still registered for updates?' Ellie threw a pad of hay towards where two of the donkeys were standing. 'People are added to those sorts of sites all the time.'

'I set up a separate email address for it, because Ollie wanted to make sure no one could keep contacting me if I didn't want to respond to any of the matches I might get. In case any of them turned out to be weirdos. So I haven't checked it for ages.'

'It's got to be worth a try, if you can remember how to access it?' Ellie scanned her face. 'I know it's a long shot and it might take a while even to work out if any new matches are related to your father, but it might just throw something useful up.'

'I'll go and log in as soon as we've finished with this lot.' Freya threw the last pad of hay into the donkeys' paddock as she spoke. Maybe modern technology would hold the key, where old photographs had drawn a blank. Someone out there had to have a genetic connection to her biological father, no matter how distant.

Logging on to the email account twenty minutes later, Freya had to marvel at how the spammers had got hold of an email address she'd only ever used for one purpose. There were offers to buy Viagra, chat with sexy singles in her area and to earn money in some kind of pyramid scheme. As she filtered the messages to see if there were any from the genealogy website, her heart sank. The only messages from them were advertising additional services and offers to trace her family tree, but for that you at least needed the most basic of information: who your parents were.

What she hadn't noticed at first were a whole group of messages amongst the spam from the same email address – Ollie's email address. The first one was dated two days after she'd confronted him and Sophie in the restaurant.

✉ Email from ollieking2@digiterweb.com

I've tried every way of getting hold of you. You've blocked my calls and my emails from your usual account, so I'm trying this in the hope you might still be checking and that you'll see this message. I'm so sorry. I know that's not enough, but I promise you that meeting Sophie without telling you had nothing to do with wanting to hide anything from you. I just hated the thought that if you knew the truth about what she wanted, you'd feel it was one more person you'd lost from your life. It kills me how much loss you've already had to go through and I wanted to try and keep your friendship with Sophie intact. I can see that was stupid now, but I hope to God you can forgive me for being stupid, because that's all I've been. I love you so much, Freya, and I don't know how to even begin imagining a life without you in it. Please call, I'll meet you wherever you want and do whatever it takes, just give me a chance xxxx

There were more messages after that, every day up until the date of the wedding, but then they'd stopped dead. She hadn't read any more after the first one, partly because tears were blurring her eyes and partly because she couldn't bear to read what else he had to say. The evidence kept stacking up that she'd been horribly wrong and the only way she could cope was by ignoring it, because the alternative didn't bear thinking about. Losing part of her connection to John was devastating, but that hadn't been her fault. If losing Ollie was all down to her, then she'd hurt the kindest man in the world for no good reason.

* * *

'Remind me how we got roped into this again.' Ellie was finding it increasingly hard to slip her bump out from behind the steering wheel without the aid of a greasing agent.

'I'm not sure, but sometimes I think women's lib has a lot to answer for.' Liv held the door of the truck open for Ellie, as Freya stood behind her, still looking worryingly pale. She'd confided when they'd fed the animals that morning that the hunt for her father, using a photo that wasn't even him, had been a complete wild goose chase as a result. Ellie just hoped that revisiting the DNA database might give her some kind of clue to go on.

'Do you really feel up to helping out, Freya? I'm sure Julian and his wife can give us a hand moving the bales if we need them to.'

'I'm fine. I think doing something instead of sitting around, over-thinking everything, will be good for me. Helping out with the events at the farm, is the only thing that's been keeping me sane.'

'Well you won't have time to think for the next couple of days, until after the fundraiser, if that helps.' Ellie felt a sharp kick under her ribs as she spoke, and put a hand on her stomach. 'I think this one has got the hump that he'll be missing out on the big Christmas party.'

'You're the one who should be taking it easy.' Freya turned to Liv, looking for support.

'Absolutely, but when you've known Ellie for as long as I have, you'll realise she never asks someone to do what she isn't willing to do herself. But if you can manage to hold her in a headlock, while I load the truck up with straw bales, we might just be able to get her to take it easy.' Liv pulled a face.

'I'm perfectly capable of lifting a couple of bales of straw; I'm pregnant, not sick. And, with the Agri-Rescue Christmas party out of the way, there's nothing left after the fundraiser until the New Year. So I can relax after tomorrow.'

'Yes, but there's already a lot of strain on your back. And it's my medical opinion that you should take on supervisory duties only, for today. In fact, if you don't, Liv and I are both going to go on strike, aren't we?'

'Definitely. And Freya's a hospital sister, so you've got to do as she says or you might not just hurt your back, you'll hurt her feelings too.' Liv knew her far too well, after a friendship that dated back almost to the beginning of her life, and she also knew exactly what to say to get Ellie to co-operate. The last thing she wanted was to contribute even the tiniest extra bit of additional hurt to Freya, even if Liv only meant it as a joke.

'Okay, but I'm going to get Julian to give you a hand too. Ben and Alan already feel bad enough about letting us down, but if we don't get the bales today, we're not going to have time to set everything up.' Ellie tapped her bottom lip, running through the list of a million things, in her head, that they needed to have ready for the Christmas fundraiser the following day. The wedding barn was being set up as the venue for the party, and they needed the bales of straw to use in the nativity scene, and for seating around the edge of the barn, so that it had the rustic look they were going for. Alan and Ben had planned to head over and pick them up, but Ben's locum had come down with a sickness bug, leaving the surgery without any cover.

On top of that, Alan had rushed off – just as they were about to leave the farm – to take Karen back into the hospital when she'd started to get a dull ache in her leg. Freya had reassured them that it was probably just part of the recovery, but she'd insisted that Karen should get it checked out, on the slim possibility that it was a sign of something more worrying, like a deep vein thrombosis. None of them had actually said that last part to Alan, but just the mention that Karen might need checking out had been enough to send Ellie's stepfather running for his car keys. She was lucky to have him, they both were. And, like Freya, she was glad to have something to take her mind off things, to stop her checking her phone every five minutes, to make sure the hospital had given her mum the all-clear.

Julian London was one of Ben's closest friends, and he ran Coppergate Farm which was a few miles outside of Kelsea Bay. Rescuing a disabled sheep from his farm was one of the things that had brought Ellie and Ben together, so she had a soft spot for Julian and his family.

'Let's head up to the farmhouse and see if anyone is about.' Ellie strode across the yard, which, as part of a working farm, was much less picturesque than the one at Seabreeze. Her yard looked more like something out of movie set, since they'd made it wedding ready. They still had quite a few animals, but no bride wanted to pick her way across a muddy farmyard, with potholes the size of paddling pools filled with dirty water. Julian clearly had no such qualms, and he sent up a spray from the puddles as he skidded to a halt just in front of them, on his quad bike.

'Ah, it's the workers!' Getting off his bike, he strode towards them. He had a typical farmer's complexion, ruddy and weather beaten, and hair that looked like it didn't see a brush on a daily basis. 'Caroline's had to go to a recorder concert that Maisie's in, but I volunteered to stay behind and help you with the bales. There are no flies on me!'

'I'm sure she'll record it on her phone for you.' Ellie couldn't help laughing at the look on Julian's face. 'And then you can watch it over, and over, and over again.'

'She wouldn't do that to me, would she? It's supposed to be the season of goodwill to all men!'

'I know I would, if I were her.' Ellie turned to the others. 'Julian, this is Freya, a friend who is trying out The Old Stables for us, before we start letting it out on a regular basis next year, and of course you know Liv.'

'Good to see you both; I hope you know what you're in for. There'll be no need to visit the gym this week.'

'I knew there had to be some upside.' Liv didn't sound like she believed what she was saying, and Freya still wasn't saying much at all. Ben told Ellie he'd asked Julian whether he knew who Freya's dad might be, but that was when they all thought he was the man in the picture. Ellie just hoped Freya's aunt could find out something new from her mum's old friend. Without a photo, or a definite name, they had almost nothing to go on. She couldn't help hoping that Freya's dad would turn out to be living locally, and that would give her a reason to stick around. Otherwise she might disappear out of their lives as quickly as she'd arrived in them, and Ellie had to admit she'd miss Freya when she was gone. And she wasn't the only one.

* * *

Freya might have lost her child-like appreciation of Christmas somewhere along the line, but even she could recognise what a brilliant job Ellie and her team had done of creating a festive wonderland in the wedding barn. There was an open-sided wooden shelter that Alan had put up outside the barn, which had been filled with straw and a manger, ready for the nativity scene at the end of the party. The rest of the straw bales were set out against the walls inside the barn, and there was a huge Christmas tree at the opposite end, with a strip of red carpet leading to a large wooden chair, and a sack almost as tall as the chair, which was filled with presents. Four of Ellie's team of casual staff were dressed as elves, and Alan had apparently been persuaded to take on the role of Father Christmas, after the usual Santa couldn't make it. There were rows and rows of fairy lights, tacked along the arched beams, and huge red and white gingham bows tied to the end of each arch, as well as a six-foot-high wreath hanging from the highest part of the ceiling, covered in hundreds more fairy lights, which glowed in the low light of the room. It smelt like a combination of fresh pine needles and chocolate chip cookies, and for the first time Freya actually felt like Christmas was just around the corner. Everywhere she'd gone in Kelsea Bay had reminded her of the fact, but she hadn't actually *felt* it. Christmas Day was only four days away, but it was hard to feel festive when there was no one to share everything that was wonderful about Christmas with.

'A penny for your thoughts.' Karen touched her arm as she spoke, and Freya looked down at her. Even her wheelchair was decorated for the event, with artificial strands of holly and red berries twisted around the frame of the chair, and a halo attached to an Alice band on her head.

'I was just wondering what the next year is going to bring. It's the second Christmas since I lost Mum and so much has happened in that time. This time last year, I was certain I'd be married by now. If things can turn out that unexpectedly, then maybe there's a chance that something good might actually happen in the next twelve months. Anything's possible, right?' Freya had to hold onto the tiny slither of hope she had left.

'It is. This time next year, I'll be up there with Alan, dressed as Mother Christmas if I have my way, and I'll be able to join in with the dancing, instead of sitting here, looking like an oven ready turkey.' She gestured to the silver metallic top she was wearing, as part of her angel costume. 'And I know things are going to change for you too. Why don't you go up to see Santa and tell him your wish?'

'I think I'm a bit old for all that.' If only it were that easy. 'The thing is, I don't even know what I'd wish for any more. Apart from finding out who my father is, I don't have a clue what else I want.'

'Well, you need to find somewhere to live next year, right?' Karen's tone was gentle and Freya nodded in response.

'Yes, but I wouldn't waste a wish on that... Not when it could be solved with an internet search, or registering with enough letting agents to increase my odds of finding the right place.'

'Maybe your wish should be about love, then?' Karen had barely said the words, when the sound of Ellie laughing made them both turn to look. Ben was twirling her across the empty dancefloor, making the most of it until the guests started to arrive. 'It's what I always wished for, for Ellie to find a good man like Ben to share her life with, and not have to go through what I did. Don't you want to find that for yourself?'

'I did.' Freya caught her breath, stunned, not just by the honesty of Karen's question, but the sudden realisation of just how much she'd lost. 'The truth is, I think I've already had that and thrown it away. It's taken me a long time to admit it, even to myself, but I think Ollie was telling me the truth about him and Sophie. I don't think anything was going on, except in her head. But, because of everything else that had happened, I let myself believe that something was. If my mother could lie to me, then so could my fiancé.'

'Why don't you tell him that?' Karen was forced to speak up as Christmas music began to fill the barn, but Freya shook her head.

'It's too late.' She'd barely slept the night before turning things over and over in her head and forcing herself to re-read the messages that Sophie and Ollie had sent her. What they'd said made sense, much more than the idea that Ollie could be so completely different to the person she'd thought he was. And what would Sophie get out of lying to cover for Ollie, if what she wanted most in the world was for him to be with her instead?

'It's only too late if you let it be.'

'Now you sound exactly like my auntie Linda.' Freya shook her head. 'You're both hopeless optimists.'

'There's nothing wrong with that.' Karen smiled. 'And I'd like to meet your auntie Linda, she sounds like an intelligent woman!'

'I'd like that, too.' Freya squeezed her shoulder again, as Ben opened the doors of the barn and the guests for the Christmas fundraising party started streaming in. If Christmas was a time to count your blessings, then maybe all of this had been to lead her to Seabreeze Farm – to make the new friends she was already finding it difficult to imagine her life without. There had to be some reason for it, because it didn't look like it would lead to her finding her father, before time ran out for that too.

* * *

The highlight of the Christmas fundraiser as far as Freya was concerned was a Christmas parade, involving some of Seabreeze Farm's most important residents. Gerald, the donkey who had chased Freya across the farmyard on that first day, had a starring role. Ellie walked alongside him, dressed as Mary. She was wearing what had been an old blue bedsheet just the day before, but despite still being mostly incapacitated, Karen had somehow managed to turn it into an authentic looking outfit, even if she'd protested that sewing wasn't her strong point.

Ben was on the other side of the donkey, making an equally convincing Joseph, about as far removed from the tea-towel-as-a-headdress costumes that Freya remembered from the nativity plays she'd been to as a kid. Behind them, some of the other farm animals were being led by local children, and members of Ellie's team. There was Jubilee, the newest donkey at the farm, a couple of goats, including Dolly – Gerald's accomplice on that chase across the farmyard – some sheep, a huge hairy, pink-and-black pig called Buster, and a black-and-white horse, with one blue eye and one brown eye, who Ellie had told her was called Joey. Not the traditional collection of animals from the nativity, perhaps, but with some of the children dressed as shepherds, some as kings, and a few more as angels, it felt pretty magical all the same.

'I hope Ellie doesn't go too far with the method acting as Mary and actually give birth in the stable.' Liv handed Freya a glass of mulled apple juice, her breath floating like a cloud in the cold night air, as she spoke.

'Oh God, I hope not either. She looks like she's got enough of a challenge keeping Gerald in line for now.' Freya laughed as the donkey let out a loud bray, before dropping his head into the manger and making light work of the hay lining it, knocking the doll that was supposed to be the baby Jesus on to the floor in the process. Luckily, most of the children watching were still too busy looking at the gifts, which Alan had handed out earlier, to notice. But it had given the adults a laugh.

'They'll make great parents, though, don't you think?' Liv pulled the woolly hat she was wearing down at the front. 'As long as they keep Gerald away from the baby that is.'

'Yes, that's going to be one lucky little baby.' Freya swallowed hard, clutching the warmth from the cup to her body. 'It won't just have Ellie and Ben, it'll have all of you. Imagine having someone like Karen as a grandma, wouldn't that be amazing?'

'I'm so sorry you haven't been able to find your father yet.' Liv laid a gloved hand on her arm, as tears filled Freya's eyes for what felt like the millionth time. She was sick of being someone people had to feel sorry for, and she was tired of feeling sorry for herself. But she just didn't seem able to get past it.

'I'm just being silly. I've already been lucky enough to have a great dad, so hoping for another one was greedy.'

'Of course it wasn't. You've had something great and anyone would want to find that again, if they got the chance. Are you sure there isn't someone else you should be talking to about all of this, though? Even if you don't find your dad?'

'Have you been talking to Karen?' Freya felt a stab of disappointment. She hadn't specifically asked Karen not to tell anyone else about her regrets over Ollie, but she'd assumed she'd keep it to herself, given how discreet she and Ellie had been about the reason for Freya cancelling the wedding in the first place.

'No and Karen's not the sort to gossip, but I overheard what you said to her earlier.' Liv gave her an apologetic look. 'Sorry, I know I should mind my own bloody business, but I've been where you are, and I nearly lost Seth because of it.'

'You thought he was involved with someone else?'

'Not exactly, but I almost let my past ruin our chances of making things work. You see my ex persuaded me to move all the way to Australia without mentioning one tiny detail...' Liv frowned. 'The fact that he was already engaged.'

'Oh God and I thought I had problems!' They exchanged a look and Liv laughed.

'Exactly! Anyway, to cut a long story short, I wasted years on my ex. And when I came home, I thought things with Seth were too good to be true, and that there was no way they could last. It meant I didn't tell him how I felt about him, and I didn't even tell him I wanted him to stay when he told me he was thinking about taking a job in the States. He could have moved halfway across the world without ever knowing that I loved him, and I would have lost the best thing that's ever happened to me.'

'How did you tell him in the end?' Freya wanted to know, even if she couldn't begin to imagine starting a conversation like that with Ollie and admitting that she'd got things so badly wrong. It would be too hard, and she'd be asking for rejection, especially when he'd already made it clear that it was too late.

'I didn't. Luckily he realised, probably before I was even ready to admit it to myself, and he came to tell me how he felt. It was a big risk on his part, but I'm so glad he took it.'

'I can't see Ollie turning up here and declaring his undying love. Not after the way I walked out and cancelled the wedding, without even giving him a chance to explain.' Freya was struggling to forgive herself, so couldn't expect him to forgive her either. She'd messed things up and sometimes there was just no going back, not matter how much you might want to.

'Especially as he doesn't even know where you are...' Liv scanned her face. 'But you should give him the chance. What have you got to lose? And if he really loves you, I think he'll understand that you were grieving for a dad you've never even known.'

'I don't know, I just feel like such an idiot.'

'You're far from that, and none of us want you to go. But one thing Karen did say, is that when she saw you with Ollie, when you came to look around the farm, she could tell you were made for each other.' Liv looked at her again. 'I know better than anyone how important it is not to let that slip away, but I also know you should walk away if things really aren't right. Just give him a chance. For your sake; at least that way you won't have to live with regrets.'

'I know you're right, I just don't know if I'm brave enough.'

'Yes, you are.' Liv took the paper cup out of her hand. 'And there's no time like the present.'

'You want me to do it *now*?' Freya was already shaking her head.

'If you don't do it now, you'll think about it too much and then you might never do it.'

'Why does everyone around here seem to be able to read me like a book?' Freya was already fighting the wave of nausea rising in her stomach, at the thought of picking up the phone and calling Ollie.

'It's all part of the Seabreeze Farm service.' Liv laughed again, and gave Freya a gentle nudge in the direction of The Old Stables. 'Go on, get it done, you know you want to.'

'Okay.' It was the only response Freya could manage, as another wave of nausea rose inside her. Liv and Karen were right, though; she'd never come to terms with things if she didn't at least speak to Ollie. Maybe he'd understand what he'd done when she told him about John, or maybe he'd tell her to get lost. But she had to know, and, unlike the search for her father, at least this time she knew where to start.

* * *

When you'd built yourself up to the extent that Freya had, hearing the words 'please leave your message after the tone', were distinctly anti-climactic. She hadn't been able to forget his mobile number, no matter how hard she'd tried when she'd thrown her old phone away, so dialling his number had been the easy bit. Getting him to answer had turned out to be much more difficult. She'd tried to get hold of Ollie twice more before giving up and going back to the barn to help with the post-party clean-up. Trying again for a fourth time, when she got back to The Old Stables afterwards, she'd been certain he'd pick up. Where else could he be at almost 11 p.m.? She tried not to picture him in a bar somewhere, where women, giggly with Christmas spirit of both varieties, would be only too willing to make a move on someone like Ollie.

Liv had been right; she had to know for sure whether there was any way back, even if the truth hurt her all over again and she had to accept she'd blown her chance of happiness, because she was too pig-headed to back down until it was too late. The stupid part was that it all seemed so clear now. Ollie had done everything to show her how much he loved her when they'd been together. He'd held on to her in the dead of night, when she'd cried about losing her mum. He'd been determined that she should have the wedding of her dreams, even if it meant spending a big chunk of her inheritance on it, and he hadn't made a single demand of his own. He'd worked all the hours he could to help save the deposit for the place they eventually wanted to buy in London, and for a belated honeymoon to Australia, so she could spend time with her cousin and his family. They were hardly the actions of a man capable of having an affair with her best friend, were they? It didn't make a shred of sense now that she'd had a bit of distance from it. But no matter what everyone else had said at the time, she hadn't been able to see it back then. Now she wanted what she had no right to ask for – *a second chance.*

She didn't want to leave a message, though; she had to speak to Ollie. If she left a message and he didn't reply, she might be able to convince herself that he'd missed the message somehow, and she could spend weeks on tenter-hooks waiting for him to call back. Or even worse, sending message after message until Ollie was forced to get a restraining order out against her. At least if she spoke to him, she'd know by the end of the conversation where she stood. Not having any idea where she'd be living in the New Year, or being any closer to discovering her biological father's identity, was more than enough of the unknown to be going on with.

Freya jumped as an alert pinged on her phone, nearly knocking a snoring Ginger off the sofa and onto the floor. Giving her a dirty look, the little dog rolled closer to the cushions on the back of the sofa, leaving Freya to enter the code into her phone with a shaking hand. It was stupid, she'd withheld her number on purpose, when she'd called Ollie, so it wasn't going to be from him. Her brain might be on board with that fact, but her body was still reacting as if it could be him. It was just an email alert, though, and she clicked on the icon which brought up a message from her auntie Linda.

✉ Email from linda.keaveney@digiterweb.com

Hello Lovey,

Hope you are managing to have some fun with your friend. I really wish you were here with us, though! Denise has sent the pictures she found to your uncle Dave and I've attached them to this email. But I've found something else too. I sent Scotty a box of photos for Jen's family tree wall, and she gave me back the ones she didn't use to bring home. I was going through them with Dave and I found your mum's other journal in there, the one I thought I'd thrown out. I haven't had a chance to read it all the way through yet, but the jet lag still hasn't completely settled, so I've been reading a bit when I can't sleep. I'll bring it home with me, but if I read anything in there that I think could be a clue, I'll give you a ring. I keep hoping for a Christmas miracle and we just want you to be happy. Looking forward to speaking to you on Christmas Day, lots of love, Auntie Linda and Uncle Dave xxx

Freya opened the attachment. There were three photographs that Denise had sent through, but none of them featured her mum. There was one of what looked like a talent contest at the holiday park and she scanned the faces of the audience, wondering if her father was amongst them. Maybe he was even the guy playing the guitar on stage, or the lead singer with a mop of curly hair held back from his face by a bandana. Denise might have said he was a farmer, but Freya couldn't help wondering if even her mum's old friend *really* knew the truth. The other two photos looked like they could have been taken almost anywhere in Kelsea Bay. The small town was surrounded by farmland that blurred into the villages beyond it. One photo had a group of what she assumed were her mum's friends from the holiday park, sitting on the back of a trailer full of bales, and the other one was of a picnic on the edge of a cliff like the one at Seabreeze Farm. Maybe something in the background of one of the photographs would be more significant to Karen, or one of the others, but there was still no light bulb moment of recognition for Freya. She was sure she'd know her father when she saw him, but no one in any of the pictures made her feel anything other than disappointed.

She wanted to believe that the journal would be the thing to turn up the vital clue, to a secret that seemed to have been buried forever with her mother. But if the search so far was anything to go by, then they really did need a Christmas miracle. Call it self-preservation, but she wasn't building up her hopes. Dialling Ollie's number again, it went straight to voicemail and this time she forced herself to say something and leave her new details. He had her number now; the ball was in his court. It looked like Auntie Linda was going to have to revise her order and put in a request for *two* Christmas miracles, but Freya wasn't holding out much hope for either of them.

10

The first Christmas miracle at Seabreeze Farm appeared in the shape of a snow shower two days after the fundraising party, and only a couple of days before Christmas itself. There'd been an article earlier in the week, giving odds of eighty to one on an official white Christmas. All that meant was that a single snowflake would have to fall somewhere in the country on the twenty-fifth of December. The weather was bucking the pessimistic prediction pretty spectacularly, especially as the southeast was usually the last place in the country to get snow, not the first. It wouldn't last long enough to fleece the bookies, though, everyone said so, and the business of running Seabreeze Farm couldn't stop as a result of a couple of flurries of snow. Although Ellie's pregnancy seemed to be making everyone just that little bit more cautious.

'I can give the farmer's market in Elverham a miss if you want. I don't like the idea of the two of you being home alone if anything happens with the baby.' Alan's voice was gruff, a dead giveaway that he was concerned.

'Thanks, but it's the busiest market of the whole year and we'll be fine on our own, won't we, Mum?' Ellie had to suppress the urge to smile. Alan was the best stepfather anyone could ask for, but even his talents didn't extend to midwifery – at least not of the human kind. If she'd been a sheep, it might have been a different matter. They lived on a farm, but it wasn't what you'd call remote, and the nearest midwives were only based about twenty minutes away. Not that she had any intention of having a home delivery; she'd seen enough births in her time on the farm to know that human beings were very lucky to get the amount of pain relief they had available, and Ellie was planning on making use of it all.

'I'll head back if the snow suddenly gets a lot worse.' Alan picked up his keys. 'Not that it will; I don't think I can remember a white Christmas down here for at least thirty years. But with Ben out on call, I won't be taking any chances.'

'All right, Dad!' Ellie had used the term jokingly a couple of times, when Alan had laid down the law before, if he was trying to persuade her to do what he thought was best for her. This time something flickered across his face, but she was never quite sure if he was pleased or uncomfortable when she called him that. She'd been thinking for a while about what the baby might call him, when it eventually learned to talk, and now seemed as good a time as any to bring it up. 'Do you mind me calling you Dad?'

'I know you're only teasing me.' Alan's face had flushed red all the same, and Ellie silently prayed that she wasn't embarrassing him. 'I've heard you say "all right Mum" to Liv, too, when you think she's bossing you around about slowing down.'

'That's how I meant it at first.' Ellie glanced at Karen, before turning back to Alan, wondering if she should have discussed it with her mum first, but it was too late now. 'I've just been thinking over the past few weeks that I'd like the baby to call you Granddad. And, you know, maybe it would just avoid confusion if I called you, er, erm...'

'*Dad*?' Karen completed the sentence she'd been struggling to finish.

'Yes, but only if you're okay with it.' It was Ellie's turn to feel the heat rise up her neck. Maybe Alan wouldn't want it, and now she'd put him in a really awkward position.

'Oh Ellie, are you sure?' His voice caught, and she nodded. 'Of course I'd love that, but won't it feel awkward for you?'

'I think I can get used to it, if you can?'

'I honestly don't know what to say.' Alan didn't need to say anything, because his face was already revealing exactly how he felt.

'Give me a hug instead then.' Ellie stepped into his arms, turning her head when she heard Karen start to cry.

'Mum, what's the matter?'

'It's just so lovely and I want to get up there and hug you both, but I'm stuck in this bloody thing!'

Ellie looked up at Alan, as she pulled away, and they both moved over to Karen's wheelchair, putting their arms around her on either side.

'Feel better now?' Alan's tone had steadied, but Karen was still sniffing as she nodded in response.

'It's just you're the two people I love most in the world, and I couldn't have asked for more than this.' Karen gave another sniff. 'I don't know how you're going to top this, though. There isn't anything I could get for Christmas that would mean a millionth as much.'

'She could have the baby.' Alan laughed, as Ellie shook her head.

'Nope, I'm holding on to this little one until the New Year, so its grandma can be there when I do give birth.'

'Good point, and it definitely won't top this, but being told I can get rid of this wheelchair for Christmas would be pretty amazing.' Karen squeezed the place where Ellie's waist had long disappeared. 'The district nurse is coming up later, so hopefully she'll give me the go ahead to get up on my feet more and more, now that the top half of the cast is off.' Alan had taken her to the hospital, the day after the fundraiser, and they'd told her the femur was now stable enough for that part of the cast to be removed, largely because of the fact that the bones had been pinned back together in an operation straight after the accident. She'd been hoping that they'd let her have a boot for the tibia break, which was taking longer to heal, but they'd just replaced the full leg cast with a half-leg cast instead. Even Liv's offer to decorate it with holly and berries hadn't managed to cheer her up when she'd first got home.

'Just hold off until I get back, though, okay?' Alan looked at both of them as he spoke, and Ellie wasn't sure if he meant her, or Karen. As it turned out, only one of them would be able to keep their promise.

* * *

Freya had continued to walk Ginger, but since the seagull hunt had almost ended in disaster, she wasn't risking letting the dog off her lead any more. With the snow still coming down quite quickly, she'd decided against a walk on the beach. The road down to the bay was quite steep, and slipping and sliding their way down there, and back again, meant the beach didn't hold its usual appeal. The snow finally looked as though it was slowing down to a gentle flurry, as Freya headed towards the patch of woodland where Ellie's farmland narrowed to a point, like the tip of a triangle. Ginger seemed to be quite enjoying the feel of the snow under her paws, and she was bouncing in and out of the potholes in the rough terrain, like Tigger on a mission. Under the cover of the woodland, Freya had realised it was snowing again, but she'd had no idea how heavily until they'd emerged from the trees. Everywhere was covered in white, and she could barely make out where the cliff edge was any more. The fence posts that supported the wires, separating Ellie's farm from Alan's, were already half-buried under the snow, but Freya was careful to stick close to the fence, so there was no risk of her or Ginger accidentally plunging down the side of the cliff. Every step back towards the farmhouse felt like they were wading through a waist-high swamp. By the time they got there, Ginger had clumps of snow sticking to the fur on her belly, and Freya's waterproof coat was the only thing that stopped her being soaked to the skin.

'Oh thank God.' Karen was sitting in her wheelchair, in the open doorway of the farmhouse, when Freya got back to the farmyard.

'What on earth are you doing sitting there, with a

freezing cold wind blowing in the house?' Opening the gate, Freya headed straight up the path.

'I managed to open the door with Aunt Hilary's old walking stick and I was keeping an eye out for you.' Karen was shaking, and Freya had a horrible feeling it wasn't just because of the cold. 'Ellie won't let me call an ambulance, but her waters have broken and both the on-call midwives are stuck out on the roads. I can't get hold of Alan or Ben, and I'm bloody useless like this!' Karen slammed a fist against the side of the wheelchair.

'It's all right. Let me have a look at her and we can work out how urgent it really is. If she's not having contractions yet, or they're a long way apart, there's no need to worry. First babies usually take quite a long time to come anyway.' Freya hoped she sounded more knowledgeable than she felt. She might be a trained nurse, but her experience of delivering babies was limited to say the least.

'I'm so glad you're here, Freya, I don't know what I'd have done without you. Neither of us want to call an ambulance if it isn't needed yet, but I just can't bear the thought of anything happening to Ellie or the baby.'

'It won't, I promise.' Closing the front door behind her, and with Ginger at her feet, Freya followed Karen back down the corridor.

'Ooohhh.' The sound Ellie was making was a dead giveaway, before Freya even saw her friend, who was panting on all fours in the sitting room of the farmhouse.

'How often are the contractions coming, Ellie?' Freya waited as the other woman shook her head, clearly unable to speak until the worst of the pain had passed.

'About every five minutes I think.' She sat back on to her haunches as she finally spoke.

'We need to time them, so we can be sure, and track whether they're getting closer together. Either way we need to call an ambulance, as it might take a while, especially in this weather.' Freya racked her brains, trying to remember what she'd been taught about childbirth during her training. It was a long way from the cardiac ward, and suddenly being faced with a patient with acute angina seemed like a far less daunting prospect.

'I don't want you to call an ambulance, unless it's an absolute necessity, okay? Like Mum said before, if we call one out when we don't really need one, they could be helping someone with a real emergency instead.'

Freya shook her head. 'I really think you should call one, because there's always a chance that things could progress and I'd much rather err on the side of caution than leave it too late.'

'I'm sure one of the midwives will make it up here before too long and let me know if I need to go into the hospital. Ben will be home soon and he can take me there in the four-by-four.' Ellie was adamant, but the clue to her determination was in the last thing she'd said. She didn't want to go anywhere without her husband.

'You might not have time to wait for Ben.' If Karen could have paced in a wheelchair, Freya was certain she would have done.

'First babies take ages.' Ellie was already wincing again, and Freya watched her face. If this was another contraction, then promise or no promise, they were going to have to call that ambulance.

'Are you having another pain?' Freya spoke as calmly as she could; she didn't want Karen to panic any more than she already was.

'No, it's just my back.' Ellie screwed her face up and Freya hoped she wasn't lying.

'Do you want me to rub your back for you?' She moved over to where Ellie was crouched.

'Yes please. No offence, but I wish Ben was here.'

'So do I.' Karen and Freya spoke at the same time, and exchanged a half-smile as Ellie dropped back down on to all fours.

'You're contracting again, I can feel it, and that was much less than five minutes.' Ellie's muscles were visibly contracting, even if she was trying to hide it. 'I'm sorry Ellie, but we're going to have to get an ambulance up here, unless you want to have this baby at home.'

'Nooooooo.' It sounded more like a moo than an answer, as another contraction gripped Ellie's body.

'Come on, sweetheart, don't be silly. You need an ambulance and I'm going to call one. I'd like to say I'm putting my foot down, but it's another thing I can't do while I'm stuck in this chair.' Karen was already dialling the number.

'What if it takes me to the hospital and I have the baby before Ben gets there.' As the contraction eased off, Ellie was able to speak again, but there were tears running down her face that had nothing to do with the pain.

'You won't be able to stop this baby for Ben, or anyone else, if it's ready to come. The best thing you can do is to get to the safety of the hospital and we can ring Ben to let him know. The way the roads are, it'll probably be safer and quicker for him to go straight to the hospital anyway.' Freya was still rubbing Ellie's back when Karen came off the phone. It had been impossible to hear all of what Karen had said, with Ellie trying to pant away the pain. What a ridiculous expression that was; it must have been a man who'd come up with that.

'They're going to get an ambulance out here as soon as possible, but it's pretty busy with the roads as bad as they are, and there's been a seven car smash on the motorway, so the operator said.' Karen held up her palms and shot Freya a worried look. 'We just have to sit tight and carry on doing what we're doing. I've texted Ben and Alan again, to let them know what's going on. There's not much else we can do.'

'Is there any more news on your dad? Or matches on the DNA site?' Ellie turned her head towards Freya as she stretched her arms out in front of her, in what would have looked like a downward dog yoga pose, if she hadn't been quite so heavily pregnant.

'Don't worry about that for now. You've got enough to think about, without being concerned about me.'

'Please tell me about it; it'll help take my mind of things until the ambulance gets here.' Ellie was almost pleading.

'There weren't any new matches on the DNA database, but Mum's old friend sent me a few more pictures through. I was going to bring them over later so you could take a look to see if there's anyone you might recognise.'

'Go and get them now.' Ellie's tone was still insistent, but there was no way Freya was leaving her to go and get the pictures.

'Don't be silly, there'll be plenty of time to look at them, after this little one arrives.'

'Please! Tell her, Mum, tell her it's okay to go and get

them. If I don't think about something else, I'm going to start really panicking that Ben's about to miss the birth of our first baby, and I couldn't bear that.'

'I think you should do it.' Karen nodded at Freya as she spoke. 'It won't do her any good getting into a state about Ben. Just don't leave us for any longer than you have to.'

'Ooomph,' Ellie grunted as she moved back on to all fours and tried to straighten the dip in her back.

'I'll go after this one's over and I'll be straight back, I promise.' Freya waited until the tension had drained from Ellie's face again, and reset the stopwatch on her Fit Bit. There was no denying how close together the contractions were now, and Ellie wasn't the only who needed distracting from the panic.

* * *

'It's definitely the tractor from Alan's farm in the picture, I ought to know. When we first met, his dresser was filled with photos of tractors he'd had over the years, like other people have photos up of their family and friends.' Karen laughed as they chatted in a brief break between Ellie's contractions, which were down to about every sixty seconds. Ben had rung to say he was on his way back from his friend Julian's farm where he'd been operating on an injured ewe.

'There's a good chance Alan might recognise someone in one of the photos then, if they were on his farm.' Freya almost had to regulate her own breathing, along with Ellie's. The prospect that Alan might be able to give her the first genuine clue to finding someone who knew her father, was almost too good to be true.

'If they helped with the harvest, then I should think he almost certainly knew who they were. They were a bit funny, him and his parents, not great mixers if you know what I mean. So visitors to the farm would almost certainly have stuck in their minds.'

'Can I have another look, oh no, wait. Oooohhh.' Ellie dropped her head down again. The gap between the contractions was closer to thirty seconds this time.

'Do you think we should give the ambulance another call?' Freya looked at Karen, who nodded. Both of them realised that if the ambulance didn't get here soon, it wasn't just Ben who'd miss the birth.

'I'll call them now.' Just as Karen reached out to pick up the phone, it began to ring, and all Freya could hear was one side of the conversation that followed. 'Hello, yes, that's right... Please tell me you're joking... No, no, of course not, sorry... We can't wait for that. I don't think she's going to make it for much longer... I can't, I'm in a wheel-chair.... No, we've got our friend here, she's a nurse actu-ally... Right, yes, I'll hand you over.' Karen held out the phone to Freya and her heart began thudding against her chest. She might only have heard one half of the conversa-tion, but she already realised this was going to be down to her.

'Hello.'

'Hello, I'm Jilly, one of the emergency services operators, what's your name?'

'Freya.'

'Hi, Freya. I understand you've got a woman in advanced labour there?'

'Yes, her name's Ellie, and her contractions are really

powerful now. They're coming every thirty seconds. Is the ambulance on its way?'

'There is an ambulance on the way, but the one we despatched to you came off the road about two miles outside of Kelsea Bay and we need to make sure you know what to do, in case they don't make it there in time. Your friend tells me you're a nurse, is that right?'

'Uh huh, but I specialise in cardiology. This really isn't something I know much about.'

'Have you ever delivered a baby before?'

'Not on my own. I did assist with a couple, when I was on rotation during my training, but it was years ago and I barely remember anything.'

'You'll be fine, Freya, just carry on doing what you are doing and keep calm for me. Okay?'

'Okay.'

'I need to push!' Ellie shouted and Freya's promise to keep calm immediately dissolved.

'She's saying she wants to push.'

'Okay, well you need to get prepared, just in case she's ready to push. But see if you can get Ellie to slow down until the paramedics can get there. Ask her to keep repeating this – three pants and one long blow – it might ease off the urge to push. Then ask her to get on all fours and bring her chest up to her knees, with her face towards the floor, and her bottom in the air. It sounds silly but it might slow things down.'

Freya passed on the operator's instructions and Ellie did her best to follow the advice, but her face kept twisting in pain every time she looked up.

'Is there anyone else there with you? Apart from the lady

I spoke to, who's in the wheelchair?' The operator's voice was still calm, and Freya briefly wondered what sort of training you had to go through, to perfect that gentle lilt, in the face of a crisis like this.

'No, just me.'

'Okay then, Freya, I take it you've already got the place nice and warm with the heating on and everything?'

'Yes, it's really warm.' Maybe it was the panic making Freya sweat, but being cold was one problem they weren't going to have.

'That's good. Right, now, tell Ellie to keep repeating the panting whilst you go and get these things as quickly as you can. You'll need something to cover the floor if you can find it, some clean towels for the baby, a blanket and a large bowl.'

Freya didn't think she'd ever moved so fast in her life, but it was hard when you were in someone else's house and you had no idea where anything was kept. By the time she got back to the room, Ellie had returned to her original position, and Karen, who'd been talking to the operator, almost threw the phone at her.

'Okay, I've got everything, but Ellie looks like she's pushing. I don't think she's going to be able to pant this baby away!' Freya's voice rose, but she was almost drowned out by the noise of a tractor sounding its horn outside the farmhouse window.

'It's Ben.' Ellie's face relaxed for a few seconds, before the grimace was back. And sure enough, Ben came running into the sitting room five seconds later, with Julian just behind him.

'The baby's dad is here.' Freya wasn't sure why, but she felt the need to tell the operator that Ben had just arrived.

'I take it he's not a doctor?'

'Unfortunately not, but he is a vet.' Freya couldn't help laughing.

'Well, you should be fine between the two of you then.' The operator broke her calm demeanour for just a moment to laugh as well. 'But I'll stay on the line to talk you through, just in case.'

Freya watched as Ben leant over his wife, and whispered into her ear, before kissing the top of her head and holding on to her hand. Julian had disappeared into the kitchen on the pretext of making tea, as soon as he'd caught sight of Ellie, and Freya couldn't say she blamed him.

'It's coming, I can feel it.' Ellie pulled down on Ben's arm as she shouted.

'Did you hear that? Ellie said the baby's coming!'

'Yes, I heard her.' The operator's voice was almost hypnotic. 'Can you have a look to see if you can see the baby's head?'

'Umm, okay.' Freya tentatively lifted up the blanket she'd laid across Ellie's knees, just before Ben and Julian had burst in. 'Oh God, yes, there's definitely a head.'

'That's good. Now, fold one or two of those towels in half and put them under Ellie's bottom, so that the baby has a soft landing if you don't manage to catch it.'

'You want me to catch it?' Freya's adrenaline was in over-drive and she was definitely in flight or fight mode – although at that moment, flight sounded far more appealing.

'If you can, but you're going to have to keep a firm hold of it.'

'I don't know if I can, I...' Glancing back at Ellie, Freya took a deep breath, as her friend let out another scream. Ellie didn't have a choice about getting through this, and neither did she. 'Okay, the head's out.'

'Brilliant. Now tell Ellie to keep panting, and if you can, see if you can loop the cord over the baby's head. And then it's just the last push.'

'The operator said to keep panting, Ellie, you're doing brilliantly.' Freya did as she was told, releasing the pressure on the cord. 'Okay, when you're ready you can push again.'

In the end it was so quick that Freya almost didn't manage to keep hold of the baby, but somehow she did, wrapping the little girl in a soft towel and placing her gently on Ellie's chest.

'It's a girl, isn't it? After all those months of us being convinced it would be a boy!' Karen was crying so much, she could hardly get the words out.

'Yes, and she looks perfect as far as I can see.' Freya lifted the phone back up to her ear. 'It's a girl, and she's pink and crying almost as much as the rest of us.'

'Perfect. You did a great job.'

'Thanks Jilly, I think I might have gone to pieces without you.'

'No problem. Give my congratulations to Mum and Dad and I'll stay on the line until the paramedics arrive, just in case you need me. But you can put the phone on the side and just let me know when the ambulance gets there, if everything seems okay.'

'Thank you so much.' Freya put down the phone, and the baby stopped crying as Ellie stroked her head.

'If you think you're paying for your stay in The Old

Stables, Freya, you can think again.' Ellie was half-laughing and half-crying, the shock of the baby coming so quickly taking hold.

'Too right. In fact you can stay here for nothing whenever you like.' Ben grinned at her, and she had a feeling he wouldn't stop smiling for months.

'And I'll make you a cake whenever you want one. Not much in the big scheme of things, but nothing would ever be enough to say thank you.' Karen reached out and squeezed her hand.

'I just did what the operator told me; Ellie did all the hard work. And this little lady of course.' Freya couldn't stop looking at the baby's perfect face, her tiny rosebud mouth exactly the same shape as her mum's. 'Do you know what you're going to call her?'

'No idea, I'd convinced myself it was going to be a boy. I'll just have to keep gazing at her until it comes to me.' Ellie had a look of blissful exhaustion, as Ben gently swept the hair away from her face. 'I think I should get to pick as I did all the hard work, and Ben gets to give us both his surname anyway.'

'Whatever you want, darling.' He couldn't take his eyes off his new family, any more than Freya could stop her thoughts drifting to the man who should have been looking at her like that, on the day she was born. Wherever her biological father was, he'd missed so much already.

'Better later than never.' Karen turned her wheelchair towards the door, as the sound of an ambulance siren made the baby screw up her face.

Freya let the operator know she was free to take another call, and stood up as Ellie finally tore her eyes away from her new daughter. 'I'll leave you all to it now, but I'll come back over and see you later when you've had a bit of a chance to recover, if that's okay?'

'It's not just okay, it's an order.' Ellie smiled. 'And I meant it when I said you'll always be welcome here.'

'Thank you.' Freya shivered as she passed the paramedics on her way out to the farmyard. There were lots of promises people had made her over the years, which had proved impossible for them to keep. And for some unfathomable reason, she couldn't help feeling that this was going to be one of them.

11

_____

When Freya finally went back over to the farmhouse, after Ben had come to knock for her to insist that she join the family for dinner, and to wet the baby's head, no one would have guessed that Ellie had given birth just that afternoon. The paramedics had checked them over, and cut the cord. With both mum and baby getting the all-clear, there was no need for them to be taken into hospital. Ellie and Ben both looked amazingly comfortable already, holding the baby in their arms as though she'd always been there. The new family were all sitting together on the big leather sofa at one end of the kitchen. Julian was sitting at the kitchen table opposite Alan – obviously in no hurry to go home – and Karen had managed to get out of the wheelchair, to sit at the head of the table.

'I hope you didn't get yourself into that chair?' Freya raised a questioning eyebrow, as Karen shook her head.

'No, but the district nurse phoned to say she wouldn't be able to visit due to the weather, but that I could try to walk a couple of paces with the crutches, as long as Alan or Ben were around to help me.' She smiled. 'I've got to get going now. I can't have my new granddaughter walking before me, can I?'

'Just don't take any unnecessary risks; you've got to take it slowly.' Alan reached out and squeezed his wife's hand.

'You're a fine one to talk, love! Trudging two miles across the snow just to get back here and see the baby.' Karen shook her head and laughed.

'I'd have walked a hundred miles to meet my new grand-daughter if I had to. The van will still be in the layby in Woodyfields Lane when the snow has melted. But my grand-daughter's first day on earth will only come around once.' Alan didn't seem to be able to stop saying the word *grand-daughter*. And Freya felt another little tug at her heart, knowing she'd never quite have what Ellie did.

Seeing Ben and Ellie with their daughter was beautiful too. Maybe one day that was something Freya could have, except she couldn't picture anyone other than Ollie being the one standing next to her and, more than that, she didn't want to. They'd talked about what having children would be like and Freya couldn't just erase that image; it was so clear it was almost like a memory she'd already made. So much of the future she had envisaged with Ollie felt like that and she was lost without the roadmap they'd had all planned out.

'Can I help you with dinner?' She would have been grateful of something to do, suddenly feeling like a spare part in the middle of such a family scene. Although Julian clearly had no such concerns and was busy emptying a bowl of potato chips into his mouth, in a way that Gerald would have been proud of.

'It's all under control thank you, sweetheart. Luckily I made a big batch of lasagnes for the freezer, before I tripped over chasing that stupid sheep. Alan had put a couple of them into the oven for me, and Ben's made some garlic bread.'

'You managed to put the baby down for a minute then?' Freya smiled as Ben nodded his head.

'It was a bit of a struggle, but I suppose I can't spend my whole life just looking at how perfect Mae is, can I?'

'So you settled on a name then?' Freya caught Ellie's eye as she spoke.

'We have and we've given her a middle name too.' Ellie moved her arm, so that Mae faced out towards the room. 'Meet Mae Freya Hastings, your namesake.'

'Honestly?' Tears sprung into her eyes again, but for once they were happy ones. She had a link that would last forever now, to this wonderful family who'd welcomed her in when she'd really needed someone.

'Honestly. After what you did today, how could we not remember that in her name? You were amazing.' Ellie blew her a kiss.

'So, if it had been a boy, you'd have named him after me, right?' Julian upturned the empty chip bowl.

'I have to admit I never would have got here if you hadn't given me a lift back in the tractor. The roads were impassable, even in the four-wheel drive. I don't think it qualifies you *quite* as highly as Freya, though. But, if we ever get another dog, we'll definitely throw the name Julian into the hat!' Ben laughed, giving a casual shrug, as his friend pulled a face. 'I'm afraid you'll have to take it or leave it.'

'Well I couldn't be more honoured that you've given her

my name.' Freya finally pulled out one of the kitchen chairs and sat down.

'There's one condition, though.' Ellie gave her a serious look. 'It means you'll have to come back and visit on a regular basis.'

'Just try stopping me!' Freya couldn't stop smiling. The thought of leaving Seabreeze Farm after Christmas had added another layer to the sense of loss she was feeling, but at least now this wasn't one door that would be shutting behind her for good. 'What do you think of your new grand-daughter then, Alan?'

'She's the bonniest baby I've ever seen.' Alan smiled, but he looked a bit restless, like he might dash back out into the snow at any minute.

'Dad's just a bit nervous of holding her, he's got this idea he might break her!' Ellie laughed, and Freya was sure she'd never heard her friend call Alan 'dad' before. There was a lot changing all at once, and maybe it was just a bit over-whelming for an unassuming man like Alan.

'I've never been around babies before, you see.' Alan gave Ellie an apologetic look. 'But I'll work up courage in the end, maybe when she's not so fragile.'

'How about you, Freya, would you like to hold your namesake?' Ellie looked towards her, and Freya was up on her feet instantly. Seconds later, she was holding a brand new baby in her arms. At almost thirty-eight weeks, Mae was considered full-term, but she still looked tiny to Freya.

'How much did she weigh?'

'Six pounds and five ounces. So a lot less than the Christmas turkey Mum's ordered in!' Ellie grinned. 'You will still be joining us for dinner on Christmas Day, won't you, Freya?'

'I wouldn't want to impose.' She couldn't help wondering if she was part of the reason Alan looked uncomfortable. He'd never seemed the sort who'd be relaxed making small talk, and he'd probably be a lot happier if she and Julian disappeared.

'Don't be daft. It wouldn't be the same without you.' Karen actually wagged a finger at her. 'And Liv and Seth will be here too. You wouldn't want to miss the big proposal!'

'If you're sure, that would be great.' It had to be better than sitting around thinking about everything and *everyone* she didn't have any more. Although she'd have to make sure she kept a level head when Seth proposed. She wasn't going to spoil their big day by making it all about her and bursting into tears at the memory of Ollie proposing. She'd taken up enough of everyone's time and sympathy as it was, and if there was any chance of her making a show of herself when Seth and Liv's once-in-a-lifetime moment came, then she'd have to steer clear.

'Your photographs are up on the dresser by the way.' Karen dipped her head to one side. 'Alan and Julian have had a look, but I'm sorry, sweetheart, they don't recognise anyone in the pictures.'

Freya's heart sank, despite the fact she'd given herself a talking to about managing her expectations. She seemed to be becoming an expert at lying to herself, because the disappointment felt like a physical blow. 'I thought the photograph on the hay trailer was at your farm?' Freya handed the baby back to Ellie and walked across to the table.

'It was.' Alan's tone was tight. 'But they were probably

just kids mucking about on the back of the trailer when no one was looking. They don't mean anything to me.'

'Mum was going out with a farmer, who everyone called Giles, but her friend Denise thinks his real name was Colin. You don't remember him either?' Freya looked from Alan to Julian.

'It was a bit before my time.' Julian was munching on more tortilla chips, after Ben had re-filled the bowl. 'But I could message my dad in Spain and see if it rings any bells with him?'

'That would be great, thank you.' Freya tried to hang on to some enthusiasm, but it was as though no one in Kelsea Bay had ever heard of her father. Maybe it was time to mention her mum's name. If Julian was going to speak to his dad, he might as well have all the facts. 'You might want to tell him my mum's maiden name: it was Colleen Bright, but she used the stage name of Alannah when she was performing. Someone has to remember her, and who Giles was.'

'It was a long time ago; you might have to accept that you're never going to know who your father was, and just be thankful you had a dad who loved you.' Alan's tone was harsh. It wasn't like him to be so forceful, but her desire to find her biological father had obviously touched a nerve. He wasn't Ellie's birth dad, or Mae's biological grandfather, so it probably felt too close to home. But the difference was that they had him, and she didn't have anyone to fill the role of grandparent any more.

'I'll ask Dad if he remembers anything. Even if he doesn't know anything himself, he might be able to ask around with some of his old buddies.' Julian shoved another couple of tortilla chips into his mouth, ending the conversation.

'I think dinner should be ready, if you can get it out please, love?' Karen looked at Alan, who nodded in response, his mouth still set in a grim line. If Freya had upset him by talking about the search for her father, then she was sorry. But seeing the whole family with baby Mae had brought it home to Freya more starkly than ever. She had to know where she'd come from, if she was ever going to work out what she should be doing with her life from this point on, especially when she'd wrecked all the plans she'd had for the future with Ollie, which was the only thing she could imagine ever really wanting. But she'd been stuck in limbo for far too long already.

Freya headed back to The Old Stables after dinner, and half a glass of champagne from the bottle that had been on ice to celebrate baby Mae's arrival. It was obvious how exhausted Ellie was, and Freya had made a big thing about needing to leave them all to rest, in the hope that Julian might get the hint to go home, but he'd barely even looked up as she left. It hadn't snowed again, but the snow already on the ground wasn't showing any signs of melting, and there was a sharp bite in the air as she crossed the farmyard, with Ginger trotting along behind her. Somehow the little dog had managed to get up on the kitchen worktop, whilst everyone else was busy with the champagne toast, and had eaten all of the left-over lasagne. In disgrace and shut in the utility room by Alan, she'd been only too happy to go back to The Old Stables with Freya. Not that it had ever taken Ginger much persuading – at least Freya was someone's first choice.

Flicking on the Christmas lights, she desperately tried to get into the spirit of things and recapture that festive feeling she'd had at the Christmas fundraising party, which had all too quickly slipped away again. It was only twenty-eight hours until the twenty-fifth of December rolled around, and she hadn't written a single card or bought anyone a present. She'd wired 500 pounds to Scotty and asked him to buy everyone in the family, including himself, a gift for under their tree. Her original plan had been to get Christmas gifts for family and friends between the wedding and the twenty-fifth – delivering them at the same time as the thank you cards and photos from the wedding that never was. Her friends would understand, and she doubted Ollie or his family would welcome anything that came from her anyway. He still hadn't returned her call, but at least she knew exactly where she stood now. She wanted to get some gifts for everyone at Seabreeze Farm, though, especially baby Mae. It would be really difficult if the snow didn't clear from the roads a bit overnight, and she didn't particularly relish the idea of sledging down to Kelsea Bay, or dragging the presents back up a lethally icy road again, either.

Back on the sofa where she and Ginger seemed to spend most of their time, Freya picked up her phone to check the weather app. It didn't feel like there was much chance of it raining enough overnight to wash away the snow, but surely she was owed a bit of luck?

Typical. There was a 40 per cent chance of snow and no mention of even the vaguest possibility of rain. Clicking on her email icon, there was an alert of another message from Auntie Linda.

✉ Email from linda.keaveney@digiterweb.com

Dear Freya,

I wanted to ring and tell you this, but I couldn't get an answer and we're heading out for the day now, so I didn't want to wait until tomorrow morning your time. I found something in the journal, and I think it explains exactly who your dad is and it means you've at least got his full name now. I've typed the entry word for word below.

I'll ring you tonight (tomorrow morning your time). I hope this makes you happy, lovey. But remember, whatever happens, me and your uncle Dave love you millions.

Auntie Linda xxx

July 15th

I didn't think I'd fall for someone like Giles, or him for me come to that. We're from different worlds! The poor soul didn't know what to make of me at first, especially when I told him he had to have a nickname… How stupid would we have looked going around as Alan and Alannah, though? I need a certain image if I'm going to be spotted, and matching names with my fella doesn't cut it! He doesn't talk much, but it's kind of sexy. Brooding and stand-offish, like Patrick Swayze in Dirty Dancing. The more he acts like he doesn't want a relationship with someone like me, the more I want one with someone like him. Although he seems to have changed his mind about that lately, and he hasn't been able to keep his hands off me since we, you know… I don't think he realises he's my first and Denise said he'll drop me now I've let him have what he wants. Mind you, he won't have anything to do with the gang from work, it's just me and him, or nothing. I don't think Denise is right, anyway. I think we're going to be star-crossed lovers, and one day I'll have a

huge singing career, but I'll come home to spend time on the
farm with him and our big family of kids. I don't know if I'll take
his surname when we get married, Crabtree is definitely not
showbiz, but I know we're meant to be together. Just watch this
space.

'Oh Mum.' Freya hugged her knees to her chest, her
heart breaking at the innocence of her mother's words.
Denise had been right; Alan had clearly decided to dump
her mum not long after she'd written the journal entry. And
worse than that, he hadn't wanted to know about Freya
either. Not when she was a baby, and not tonight when he'd
clearly realised who she was – the daughter he'd rejected
nearly thirty years before. There she was, feeling sorry for
upsetting him, and he'd been busy rejecting her all over
again. Well, she wasn't going to be like her mum and keep
fighting for a relationship with Alan that he clearly didn't
want. Alan might have fooled her once, but she wasn't going
to let him fool her twice. He had the nice guy act down
almost perfectly, the way he'd cooed over baby Mae. No one
would have believed he'd rejected his own baby daughter,
not once but twice.

It was funny, because the more she'd got to know Alan,
the more she'd seen similarities between him and John. In
her ideal scenario, finding her biological father would have
felt the same, like there were parallels with the wonderful
father she'd spent the first fifteen years of her life with. It
was hard to believe Alan was such a let-down. From what
she'd seen of him and the way he'd helped her at the beach,
he didn't seem capable of acting as callously as he had and
Freya couldn't help thinking that he wasn't just rejecting her

as a daughter, he was rejecting her as a person. He'd clearly opened his arms to Ellie, but Freya couldn't even compare, despite having half his DNA. She probably couldn't change his mind, even if she wanted to, and she wasn't going to beg him for a space in his life that he clearly had no intention of making. Freya liked Ellie and Karen far too much to put this on them and if Alan wanted to maintain the secret he'd already kept for three decades, then she wasn't going to be the one to drop a bombshell into his new family's life. They didn't deserve it, even if he did. She'd done what she'd come here for and found out who her father was. Now that she knew, she was ready to go and she'd be leaving Seabreeze Farm as soon as it got light – snow or no snow.

12

Ellie looked up as Ben slammed the front door. 'Did you speak to her?'

'She's not there.' He shook his head, and she could tell by the look on his face there was more bad news to come.

'She's left the keys and an envelope with your name on it. Ginger was sitting on the doormat outside in the snow, and she wouldn't come back with me either.'

Ellie handed Mae to her husband and ripped open the envelope. There was more than enough cash in it to cover the rental of The Old Stables – which they'd already told Freya she didn't need to pay – along with a hand-written note.

Dear Ellie, Karen and everyone at Seabreeze Farm,

Thank you so much for letting me stay. I don't know what I would have done without you. I'm sorry to leave without saying goodbye, but something unexpected has happened. It means I've got to leave straight away and I didn't want to wake Mae by knocking.

    Merry Christmas to you all and I wish you all the very best.

    Freya xx

'That's not a *see-you-later* letter, that's a *goodbye-forever* letter.' Ellie's throat burned at the thought, as she passed the note to Ben, whilst he cradled their daughter in his other arm. She'd already burst into tears once that morning, over some burnt toast – post-birth hormones had a lot to answer for – but this was bigger than that. They were losing someone who she'd already come to think of as a close friend and she had no idea what could possibly have made her leave so suddenly. The roads were lethal and they wouldn't even be able to check that Freya had got to wherever she was headed safely, if she didn't answer her phone. Ellie couldn't stand the thought of something happening to her while she was out there all on her own.

'I can't believe she set off in this weather.' Ben shook his head again, mirroring his wife's thoughts. 'Maybe Alan and I should head out to look for her? If something's happened with her ex to upset her, she might not be thinking straight.'

'Good idea. I'll give Mum a shout. Are you all right with the baby?' Ellie stroked her daughter's head, as Ben nodded. Karen and Alan had spent the night at Seabreeze Farm; everyone had been exhausted by the events of the day, with little Mae's dramatic entrance into the world, and she wasn't sure if her mum was up and about yet. The renovations on her parents' farmhouse wouldn't be complete until the New Year, but she knew that Alan would have been up early checking up on the animals, regardless of where he'd spent the night. Julian had finally headed off in his tractor, just before ten the night before, but the snow had been as deep as ever. 'Hopefully Alan will be ready to go straight away. I'm really worried about what might have happened for Freya to rush off like that.'

'Freya's gone?' Alan pushed Karen through the door of the kitchen, just as Ellie had been about to go and look for them.

'Yes, she went really early his morning and left a note to say that something unexpected had come up.'

'She's obviously put two and two together, and discovered the truth!' Karen gave Alan a look that Ellie didn't think she'd ever seen before.

'The truth about what?' She looked from one of them to the other, the tension between her parents tangible.

'I...' Alan turned to his wife and she folded her arms. Whatever had happened, she meant business. 'I should have said something to her yesterday, when I first realised, but I just didn't know how to do it and especially not then, in front of everyone else.'

'Okay, I know I only got about four hours sleep last night, but I have absolutely no idea what you're talking about.' Ellie's brain felt as though it was made of porridge, but her mother looked as animated as she'd ever seen her look.

'What Alan is trying to tell you, is that *he* is Freya's father.' Karen puffed out her cheeks, the only thing breaking the silence in the room. 'And instead of telling her that, and letting her know that it's a shock, but a wonderful shock, he didn't say anything at all.'

'*You're* Freya's father?' Ellie looked at Alan, trying to make sense of it. 'But I don't understand.'

'I was going to talk to her about it, I just needed time to process it and with Julian here last night, and everyone celebrating Mae's arrival, it didn't seem like the right time.' All the colour seemed to have drained from his face. 'I'd never heard the reference to Giles before yesterday, or I'd have known it was me from the beginning. It was a nickname Freya's mum gave me right after we met, and I always knew her as Alannah, not Colleen like Freya told us when she first came. When she told me about her mum's stage name, it all slotted into place. But I still couldn't quite believe it.'

'And now she thinks you've rejected her all over again.' Karen shook her head. 'No wonder the poor girl left. I've already tried her number ten times this morning and she's not picking up.'

'I didn't reject her the first time. I had no idea.' Alan looked close to tears and Ellie put her arms around him. Her mother was clearly angry, but she couldn't really believe for a moment that Alan would have rejected his daughter. He might give off a gruff demeanour to mask his shyness, but deep down he wasn't capable of hurting a fly. She knew one thing for certain, though, she'd never seen her stepfather so emotional before.

'I think you need to tell Freya that. Whatever happened back then, you've got a chance to change things now. But we don't even know what her new address is going to be, and if she changes her number again, we might not get the chance.' Ellie tried to keep the panic out of her voice.

'I'll go and look for her. This is my mess and I need to sort it out.' Alan was already pulling on his boots, which had been drying out by the wood burner.

'Do you want me to come with you, Alan?' Ben asked, handing Mae back to Ellie.

'Thanks, but I think this is something I need to do on my own.'

'Do you think we should keep trying to call her in the meantime?' Ellie looked at Alan, but he shook his head.

'She obviously doesn't want to speak to us, so I think I should try to find her and talk to her in person first.' Alan bent down to kiss Karen, and her face finally relaxed a bit. 'I'm sorry love, but I'm going to fix this. I promise.'

'Good luck, but don't come back until you've got me another daughter, because that's all I want for Christmas.'

'Me too.' Alan pulled on his coat as he spoke and Ellie knew he meant every word he said. He'd already proven to them all that he was capable of loving with the heart of a lion, and now he needed to find the courage of one, to have what could well prove to be the most difficult conversation of his life.

Finding Freya was all any of them wanted, but it wouldn't just take courage, it was also going to take a whole lot of luck for Alan to get to her before she disappeared out of their lives forever.

'I'm afraid there won't be a train until at least eleven. We've had an update and they're still trying to clear snow from the line between Kelsea Bay and Elverham.' The station assistant gave Freya an apologetic smile. 'The timetables are enough of a nightmare on Christmas Eve as it is, without adding a heavy snowfall to the problem. I hope you manage to get where you're going to.'

'Me too.' Freya shivered, pulling the coat more tightly around her body, and silently praying that she would get home by the end of the day. Not that spending Christmas in Auntie Linda and Uncle Dave's empty house was much of a home-coming, but it was all she had. She kept trying not to picture what Christmas would have been like if things were different; if her parents were still around, if she hadn't ruined things with Ollie, or if Alan had welcomed her into his family the way she hadn't been able to stop herself from hoping that her father would.

She tried not to think about what the Chapmans and Crabtrees were doing now. Knowing Ellie and Karen, they'd have been upset to get her note, but baby Mae would be taking their minds off it, and no doubt Alan would find a way of convincing them it was all for the best. By the time Christmas Day came around, they'd have already put her out of their minds and they'd never know that there was a family member missing from the place they'd set aside for her at the table. She'd never be able to forget them, even if she wanted to. But in time she'd become just an anecdote to them, a story told to baby Mae about the temporary guest who'd filled in as the midwife for her arrival and the reason for her middle name.

It didn't take long to realise that sitting on the station plat-form until eleven wasn't going to be an option. The bitter wind blowing along the tracks was sending up flurries of snow and she needed to keep moving if she was going to avoid adding frost bite to her list of problems. Glancing at her watch, she fought the urge to scream. It was still only 9 a.m. It had taken her well over an hour to get down to Kelsea Bay, and the road from the farm was still impassable by car. When she'd first turned up at the train station, at just after 7 a.m., the attendant had told her that there might be a train to London in a couple of hours. He was still saying the same thing, two hours later, and she didn't even want to think about what she would do if there weren't any trains that could get her back to Bristol, via London, before they stopped running for the day. Maybe she'd have to throw herself on the mercy of the local church; anything was better than heading back to Seabreeze Farm. Leaving had been hard enough – and Ginger had tried to follow her, until she'd shut all the gates out of the farmyard – but going back would be impossible.

Having spent two hours in the coffee shop by the station, she couldn't face anything else to drink, and she didn't relish the prospect of nursing a hot drink until it turned cold again, just to pass the time. All of the shops were open, making the most of last-minute shoppers, so she'd just have to kill time wandering around amongst the crowd. Everyone else was dashing about buying gifts for their nearest and dearest, and if she hadn't got the email from her aunt the night before, Freya would have been down there, frantically searching for gifts for everyone at Seabreeze Farm, who she had to admit had become dear to her too. At least there was no chance of bumping into any of them. They were all too busy with their own family, and the state of the road down into the bay would have put off even the most desperate of Christmas shoppers, anyway. It was easier that way; at least she wouldn't have to keep looking over her shoulder or turning every time she heard what might be a familiar voice, half hoping that one of them cared enough to come after her, despite being certain that leaving was for the best.

Freya walked past the window of Driftwood Island at least three times, before she finally went into the shop. There was no point buying Christmas decorations now, and it reminded her of her mum too much, but she seemed to be drawn in against her will all the same. The shop was almost empty, and anyone who was going to buy a Christmas decoration would have done so much earlier in December. There were a couple of people looking at the small section of the shop that wasn't filled with Christmas decorations, but it still felt like a haven of tranquillity compared to the air of panic that accompanied the bustle of the high street.

Freya's eye was caught by a driftwood wreath, which had holly leaves and berries individually carved from materials reclaimed from Kelsea Bay beach, according to the label. It was beautiful and she was staring at it, wondering if she'd ever be able to bear to look at something that reminded her of such a hard time, when someone behind her cleared their throat.

'I've been looking all over town for you, but I should just have looked in here first.' She was almost certain who the voice belonged to, but she couldn't turn around just in case she was wrong. 'I remember overhearing you that day, when we saw you in town, telling Ginger how much your mum loved this shop.'

Freya kept her eyes fixed on the driftwood wreath; she still couldn't bring herself to turn around, and she had no idea how either of them would react if she did.

'I know I've been an idiotic old fool but at least give me

the chance to explain and to tell you how sorry I am for all of this.'

She'd heard that somewhere before, someone begging her just to listen. The words were different, but Alan's sentiment was the same. She hadn't given Ollie the chance to tell her his side of things, and she'd been too pig-headed to back down until it was too late. That was one mistake she wasn't going to make twice. As hard as this was and as difficult as it might be to listen to what he had to say, Alan could have his chance. It probably wouldn't change anything, but at least no one could accuse her of not hearing him out.

'All right, but we haven't got long. I'm catching a train to London at eleven, so I can get back to Bristol in time for Christmas.' She finally turned to look at Alan and he nodded, but there was a look of desperation in his eyes.

'If that's the best I can get, then that's enough. But, before I say anything else, I need you to know this; I don't want you to leave, and neither does anyone else.'

'I'm not going to change my mind about leaving, because last night told me how things stand. But I'd be lying if there were things I didn't want to know about what happened between you and Mum, so I want us to have the chance to talk before I go. Just not here.'

'I know a place.' Alan pulled back the shop door and gestured for Freya to go through. Breathing deeply, she stepped into the street, trying to stop her legs from shaking at the thought of sitting down with her father for what felt like the very first time.

* * *

The waitress moved away from the table, after she'd set down the teapot between them, and Alan right-sided the upturned cups.

'Do you want milk?' His innocent question was another reminder that her father had no idea of even the simplest things about her, but it was time to cut to the chase.

'I just want to know why you weren't interested in me. Then, or now.' Freya's hands were knotted in her lap. She was determined not to cry in the quaint little teashop that was crowded with Christmas shoppers. Especially not with a soundtrack of *Now That's What I Call Christmas* playing in the background.

'I know you're going to find this difficult to believe, but I didn't have any idea who you were, or that Alannah was your mother, until yesterday.'

'You're right, I do find it difficult to believe.' Freya stared down at the tablecloth, which was covered with hundreds of disembodied Santa heads, all busy *Ho, Ho Ho-ing*. She felt almost as disembodied herself; whether the numbness was a result of the cold, or just her brain's attempt to protect her from any more hurt, she still couldn't quite believe she was here, sitting across from her biological father. It was almost like she was watching herself from above. 'My auntie Linda said that Mum wrote to you and told you she was pregnant, then she came down again when she'd had me and left your parents a letter to pass on to you.'

'I don't know if that's true, but if it is, then they never told me, and I didn't get either of the letters.'

'So my grandparents rejected me as well?' Freya looked up at Alan, unable to stop the tears filling her eyes despite her best intentions. She could have grown up with all of those people in her life, but none of them had wanted her.

'They'd never have done that, not if they'd known it was true.' Alan moved a hand towards her, but stopped short of putting it over hers. 'But they were frightened people. Neither of them could read or write well, and I'd already hurt them by disappearing to work on a farming project in Africa. I decided it was time to pursue my own dreams, after spending a summer with Alannah. It made me realise how small my life was, and that there was a whole world outside of Kelsea Bay.'

'You went to Africa?' Freya could hardly equate that with the man sitting in front of her, the down to earth person she'd come to know during her time at Seabreeze Farm. He seemed as wedded to the Kent countryside as he was devoted to Karen and the rest of the family.

'I wanted more than this. I don't know, maybe it was a reaction to seeing your mum go off to London to follow her dream of becoming a singer, but I felt like I was being left behind, and not just physically. I didn't think I'd ever be enough for Alannah as I was, this local yokel who couldn't compare to the exciting life she wanted to lead. I thought maybe if she came back and I could tell her I'd been to Africa, she might see me differently. So, when the opportunity came up to get involved with an irrigation project, I just wanted to do something, *anything,* to prove I wasn't a dyed-in-the-wool carrot cruncher.' Alan laughed and Freya found herself smiling through the tears.

'Is that what Mum called you?' It was yet another side to her mother that she'd never known, the same woman who'd told her that London was too scary a place to visit.

'Not exactly, but she wanted me to go to London with her and, when I said I couldn't, she said we were too different to make a go of things, and that I was too much of a country boy for her. She said we shouldn't ever have got together in the first place.'

'Is that what you think?'

'No, at least not the part about it being better if we'd never got together. Otherwise we wouldn't have had you.' Alan inched his hand closer to hers. 'But she was right when she said that we were too different and, when I was away in Africa, I let Mum and Dad down. They were targeted by a developer who ripped them off, and it made them wary of everyone and everything. If your mum told them about me, then they probably thought it was another scam. But if they'd known they had a grandchild, they'd have loved you with everything they had.'

'I wish I'd had the chance to know them.'

'Me too.'

'And what about the photo I thought was Mum, the one that turned out to be her friend? If it was a close enough likeness to fool me and Auntie Linda, didn't you ever consider the possibility that it was her?'

'There were loads of girls with that sort of haircut, but I knew, even from the small part of her face that was clearly visible in the picture, that it wasn't her.'

'How?'

'I don't know if I should be saying this, but...' Alan hesitated for a moment. 'Put it this way, I spent most of the time I was with your mum staring at her mouth. She had these amazingly full lips and a little beauty spot just above her mouth, like Marilyn Monroe. Her lips were the first thing I noticed about her, and I didn't think I'd ever get the chance to kiss her, not someone like me. I couldn't believe my luck when she asked me to go for a drink, and I'll never forget that smile, or what it felt like to kiss her. The woman in that photo had thin lips, and so I was certain it wasn't the girl I knew as Alannah. I'm sorry, you probably don't want to hear all this about me and your mum, but she was a belter and there wasn't anyone who could match her for me back then.'

'Actually, weird as it might seem, I quite like hearing it. I've been wondering, since I found out that John wasn't my biological father, if I was the unwanted result of a meaning-less fling. So the fact that you remember things like that means a lot.' Freya swallowed the lump that seemed to form in her throat every time she thought about her mum, and the fact that she'd missed the chance to *really* know the woman who'd raised her and kept such a big part of her life, and so many of her dreams, a secret.

'It wasn't meaningless and I'm glad something I said has helped. All I seem to do is get it wrong, but I never meant to hurt you. I just didn't join the dots.'

'But what about yesterday? You realised I was your daughter, then, didn't you? And you denied recognising anyone in the photographs.'

'I know and I'm sorry, but I wasn't certain if I did know them for sure. I tried to keep clear of her friends, and I always liked it best when it was just me and your mum – she seemed different then, and I could make myself believe that maybe we were suited after all. I met her friend Dee Dee a couple of times and I thought maybe I recognised her from the photo, but I still wasn't sure and I didn't really see how that could help you, anyway. I should have said something, though, and I'm sorrier for that than you'll ever realise. But I had no idea that your mum was Alannah until the moment you said it, and I was too shocked to take it in properly at first. You'd only ever called her Colleen, and she never even told me that was her real name. It was only when you told Julian that most people here knew her as Alannah that I realised it had to be me. I've spent half my life wishing I had a family of my own, and it felt like all my prayers had been answered when I met Karen and Ellie. It seemed impossible to believe that I had another daughter, and that I'd missed out on having a relationship with you for so many years.'

'I can understand what a shock that was, and I wish Mum hadn't kept it from me. But John was a good man, and seeing you with Ellie reminded me of that.' Freya dropped her gaze again. She'd reacted badly once, when someone she should have trusted had begged her to listen, but she should have believed Ollie and she believed Alan now. It still didn't make the situation straightforward. 'You've already got a family and the last thing you want is someone coming along to ruin all that.'

'Oh Freya, you've got no idea. Karen went mad when I told her what I'd realised last night, because I'd let you go home without telling her how happy I was – how happy we both are – that we've finally discovered the truth. She said, this morning, that I couldn't come back to the farm without bringing her back another daughter.'

'Another daughter?' Freya's eyes were filling up again and Alan frowned, but he clearly had no idea why she was crying.

'I'm sorry, love, I shouldn't have told you she'd said that. It's rushing you too much, and the last thing I want to do is to upset you or scare you off. We can take things as slowly as you like, as long as you give me a chance to make up for all the time that we lost.'

'You haven't upset me, and I don't want to take it slowly. We've wasted too much time already.' Freya closed the last few inches between Alan's hand and hers, until their fingers were touching. She could hardly believe this was happening and that the family she'd fallen in love with since coming to stay at Seabreeze Farm were going to be her family too. But after what had happened with Ollie, she'd promised herself she'd never throw away a chance of happiness again. 'I know what I said, about there being nothing you could say that would make me change my mind, but I'd like to come back to the farm for Christmas if you think the others would be okay with that?'

'Oh love, you've got no idea how happy that's going to make everyone. Especially me.' Alan gulped and there was no doubt in her mind that he meant every word he said. Against all the odds, and despite the best efforts of the drifting snow, she was finally going to make it home in time for Christmas.

* * *

Christmas at Seabreeze Farm was just as Freya had expected. With Karen still not as mobile as she should be, Ben took over the cooking with help from Alan and Seth. They wouldn't let Freya do anything, so she was watching *Home Alone* on the TV, with Karen, Liv, Ellie and baby Mae, and trying not to eat too many Quality Street, when the sound of a tractor engine chugging into the farmyard made Ginger start to bark.

'It's Julian.' Freya got to her feet and looked out of the sitting room window. 'And he's dressed as Father Christmas.'

'He's not dressed as Father Christmas, he *is* Father Christmas.' Ellie laughed. 'It's all right, I haven't completely lost the plot. It's just that Julian does this every year to raise money for the special care baby unit that looked after his daughter when she was born. Anyone in Kelsea Bay can make a donation to put their name on the list, and Father Christmas will bring a gift to their door. We thought we'd start Mae's Christmases off as we mean to go on.'

'What a great idea.' Freya smiled as she looked through the window again. The sides of the trailer, which the tractor was towing, had been clad with specially shaped plywood, painted in gold, to make it look like a sleigh, and it was loaded with brightly wrapped gifts. Her auntie Linda would have been beside herself with excitement if she'd been there, and it was something else Freya would have to add to the list of things to tell her about later. It was going to be one heck of a phone call.

'Ho, ho, ho!' Julian boomed out the greeting, as he walked into the house, and Mae immediately began to cry. 'Sorry, sorry, I should have been a bit less full on with the baby.'

'It's fine. We're just glad you can fit us in.' Ellie stood up and gently bounced the baby on her shoulder, which seemed to sooth Mae straight away.

'Can I get you a drink?' Ben had appeared in the doorway, with Alan and Seth just behind him, all of them wearing blue-and-white striped aprons.

'I better not, or I'll never make it to the end of my deliveries.' Julian looked them up and down and laughed. 'Looking good fellas!'

'You're just jealous, lad.' Alan followed Ben into the room and sat down next to Freya. 'But we can get you one of these for next Christmas, if you're a good boy.'

'I'm the one who's come bearing gifts, if you're ready to photograph Mae's first Christmas?' Julian put his sack down in front of Ellie and the baby, as Ben picked up his mobile phone. The whole family were in on the secret that Seth would be hiding Liv's engagement ring in her Christmas cracker later, but a visit from Santa Claus was one surprise Freya hadn't been expecting.

'Here we are, Mae, and I think there's something in here for everyone.' Julian started to hand out the gifts. 'Except for Freya. I'm really sorry, but your letter didn't make it to the elves in my workshop in time, and I didn't know you were going to be here.' Julian winked, obviously determined to stay in character.

'Ah, that's my fault Santa and I think I might be on the naughty list this year anyway.' Freya grinned. It didn't matter if she didn't have a gift, she had family to be with at Christmas and that was far more important. There was only one more thing she wanted, and it wasn't something Santa could deliver. She'd insisted that Alan let her do a bit of present shopping before they'd gone back to the farm on Christmas Eve, though, so at least she had some gifts for the others. They'd all done so much to convince her that she was part of the family now, and she was desperate to show her gratitude in some small way.

'You must have *something* on the sleigh for Freya.' Alan

looked agitated. 'It might be Mae's first Christmas, but it's my first Christmas with both my daughters too.'

'Honestly, don't worry, it's fine.' Freya didn't want him to get upset and, no matter how much they might want to, there was no way to make up for all the Christmases they'd missed out on when she was a kid. All they could do was make the most of the Christmases they could share from now on.

'I might have something. Just let me have another quick look.' Julian went back outside and Freya smiled again, as she watched Ellie unwrapping Mae's present. Ben was taking what looked like hundreds of photos of the baby's first Christmas.

'Alan was right, I think I might have found something after all.' Julian stood in the doorway. 'Or should I say *someone*.'

'Hello Freya.' As the owner of the voice stepped out from behind Julian, Freya caught her breath.

'Ollie.' She had to say his name out loud to prove he was really standing there, in front of her, and not just a figment of her imagination because she wanted to see him so desperately.

'I hope you're not disappointed, I know you usually like to get perfume at Christmas, but you'll have to make do with me instead.'

'Make do—' She seemed to have completely lost the ability to form a sentence, and she had to clamp her lips together to stop her mouth from hanging open.

'This lot clubbed together and decided I'd be the perfect gift. For some reason they seem to think I'm all you want for

Christmas and, when Ellie emailed me yesterday, she told me everything.'

'*Everything*?' Freya managed the single word and, as Ollie nodded in response, it suddenly felt horribly awkward to be having this conversation in front of everyone.

'Thank you.' She turned to Ellie, who was smiling like someone who knew for a fact that they'd just handed over the perfect present.

'What are family for? We still had a record of Ollie's work details, from when you booked the wedding, and we've probably broken every data protection rule ever written. But are we forgiven?'

'Of course but I—' She still didn't seem able to finish a sentence, and she had to fight the urge to pinch herself to make sure she wasn't dreaming. She'd picked up the phone at least ten times to try and call Ollie again, when she'd finally discovered that Alan was her father and had realised that Ollie was the one person in the world she most wanted to tell. But she'd been too afraid. He still hadn't answered the message she'd left before and she couldn't blame him. So she'd set the phone down each time, determined not to spoil her first Christmas with her new family by pining over all that she'd lost. But now here he was, standing in front of her, and she still couldn't seem to find the words she needed to stay.

'I think maybe you and Ollie should take Ginger for a walk to check whether Gerald is letting Jubilee get her fair share of their Christmas dinner, even if it is only hay. What do you think?' Ellie's suggestion was perfect.

'I think that's a great idea. Are you up for a walk?' Freya let go of a long breath, relieved that at least Ellie seemed to know what to do, and turned back to Ollie, who held out his hand in answer. Maybe Seabreeze Farm was capable of granting more than one Christmas wish after all.

* * *

Ginger ran on ahead of them, bolting towards the paddock, as Freya and Ollie crunched across the snow.

'I can't believe you're here.' She couldn't look directly at him, in case he disappeared as quickly as he'd arrived. 'How did you even make it through the snow?'

'I've missed you so much, and once I got Ellie's email, it was the excuse I needed to try again. I'd decided I was just going to work through Christmas, to make not being with you a tiny bit easier to bear. So I picked up the email as soon as it came through, and I could hardly believe everything that had happened. I'd made myself a promise that I wouldn't keep trying to persuade you to hear me out if you didn't get in touch before the wedding date. But the truth is, I never really gave up hope.' Ollie still had hold of her hand and she forced herself to look at him properly, at last. 'I called Ellie as soon as I got her message and drove through the night to get here. I've left my car in the same layby as Alan left his, apparently, and that's about as far as any car can make it. That's where Julian picked me up from, already dressed as Father Christmas. It's all been a bit surreal! Especially as I wasn't sure if I'd ever see you again.'

'I rang you a couple of times, and left you a message, but you never got back to me. Not that I expected you to, after what I'd done.'

'I changed my number after you left as Sophie started to

bombard me with calls saying she needed to talk. I said I didn't want to, that there was nothing else to say, and I even blocked her number, but she'd just call me from work, or her parents' house, or from a friend's place. In the end it just seemed easier to change my number altogether. When your auntie Linda told me you wouldn't even consider talking to me, I figured the last thing you'd want was my new number and somehow it made the disappointment easier to handle, knowing it couldn't be you when the phone rang. Instead of hoping it was and then getting a punch in the gut when it wasn't. I think Sophie wanted me to tell her that I forgave her for breaking us up, but I couldn't do that, because I couldn't forgive her when I'd lost the only thing I ever wanted: a life with you.'

'But you can forgive me?' It seemed incredible that he was even there, after everything Freya had put him through.

'I love you and I could have forgiven you, even if I didn't know what had happened that morning and how much finding out about your dad must have affected you.' He turned her to face him, as Ginger started bounding back across the snow towards them, and she had to ask him the question that had kept her awake so often.

'When I saw you and Sophie together, it looked so much like there were real feelings between you. I just couldn't believe there was any other explanation, and it took me a long time to admit to myself that I might have been projecting how I felt about being lied to by Mum on to you.'

'The timing couldn't have been worse. If it had been ten seconds later, all you'd have seen was me walking away from the table. I told her that was it, and it was the last time I'd meet her. I made it clear she couldn't keep emotionally blackmailing me, by threatening to hurt herself. It had to stop; I love you and nothing was ever going to happen with Sophie. I felt sorry for her and I let things she said and did go because I was trying to make it easier for her, but I should have pulled back from our friendship straight away. I handled it all really badly. So the question is, do you forgive me, for not telling you about how Sophie felt about me, as soon as she told me? And for handling the whole thing like a complete idiot?'

'How about we call it quits?' Freya was still half expecting him to tell her she must be joking, and that he'd never be able to forgive her for overreacting and calling off their wedding the way she had.

'It's a deal.' Watching his face as he spoke, she was more certain than ever that he wasn't trying to deceive her about anything, and that he never had been. It was the same sense of certainty she'd had that Alan was telling the truth, when he'd told he hadn't known he'd had a daughter. There were just some things that couldn't be faked.

'I've missed you, Ollie King, more than you'll ever know.'

'Oh, I think I know, but I'd be willing to let you show me...' Just as Ollie was about to kiss her, Ginger skidded to halt by their feet, sending up a shower of snow.

'Someone's trying to ruin the romantic moment.'

'Bigger things have tried that before and they've all ended up losing.' Ollie bridged the gap between them again as he finally kissed her.

'Merry Christmas, Ollie.' She whispered the words when they eventually broke apart.

'Merry Christmas, Freya. I need you to know that nothing's changed for me, it never did – I still want to marry you, here, just like we planned. As soon as you think you're ready.'

'I think that can be arranged at some point.' Freya laughed as Ginger sped off again, sending up another shower of snow. 'And this time I think we might even qualify for a family discount!'

ACKNOWLEDGMENTS

I hope you have enjoyed the second novel in the *Seabreeze Farm* series. Although I don't own a donkey sanctuary, I was born a stone's throw from the cliffs that overlook the English Channel. I also grew up on a small holding, where taking in stray animals was a fairly regular event and, by the time I'd left home, I'd done everything from covering the night shift feeds for abandoned lambs to delivering a foal with nothing more than the aid of an Encyclopaedia Britannica – long before the days of Google! So I've drawn upon a lot of personal experiences to write the *Seabreeze Farm* series and it's very close to my heart as a result.

This book is dedicated to the wonderful Peter Glanvill. Sadly, Peter is no longer with us, but both he and his wonderful wife, Maureen, have been like family to us from the day we met them. Peter was the epitome of what all good fathers should be and he did an amazing job of filling the vacancy of granddad in the lives of my children, after both their grandfathers died before they were born. We all still miss Peter, but his memory lives on and I don't think I ever saw him without a smile on his face.

The support for my books from bloggers and reviewers so far has been incredible and I can't thank them enough. To all the readers who choose to spend their time and money reading my books, and especially those who take the time to get in touch, it means such a lot to me and I feel so privileged to be doing the job I love.

Thanks too to all the subscribers to my newsletter; if you haven't signed up yet you can find the link on my Twitter account and Facebook author page. There are lots of opportunities to enter competitions and contribute to the books by naming a character or, in the case of the *Seabreeze Farm* series, an animal! You'll also receive exclusive free short stories from time to time too.

My thanks as always go to the team at Boldwood Books for their help, especially my amazing editor, Emily Ruston, for lending me her wisdom to get this book into the best possible shape and set the scene for the next book in the series. Thanks too to my wonderful copy editor and proofreader, Candida, for all her hard work. I'm really grateful to Nia, Claire and the rest of the team for all their hard work behind the scenes and especially for marketing the books so brilliantly, and to Amanda for having the vision to set up such a wonderful publisher to work with.

As ever, I can't sign off without thanking my writing tribe, The Write Romantics, and all the other authors who I am lucky enough to call friends.

Finally, as it always will, my biggest thank you goes to my family – Lloyd, Anna and Harry – for their support, patience, love and belief in the years it took to get to this point. I love you all, and baby Arthur, more than you'll ever know.

MORE FROM JO BARTLETT

We hope you enjoyed reading *Finding Family at Seabreeze Farm*. If you did, please leave a review.

If you'd like to gift a copy, this book is also available as an ebook, digital audio download and audiobook CD.

Sign up to Jo Bartlett's mailing list for news, competitions and updates on future books.

http://bit.ly/JoBartlettNewsletter

Why not explore the top 10 bestselling The Cornish Midwives series:

ABOUT THE AUTHOR

Jo Bartlett is the bestselling author of nineteen women's fiction titles. She fits her writing in between her two day jobs as an educational consultant and university lecturer and lives with her family and three dogs on the Kent coast.

Visit Jo's Website: www.jobartlettauthor.com

 twitter.com/J_B_Writer
 facebook.com/JoBartlettAuthor
 instagram.com/jo_bartlett123

Boldw⌾⌾d

Boldwood Books is an award-winning fiction publishing company seeking out the best stories from around the world.

Find out more at www.boldwoodbooks.com

Join our reader community for brilliant books, competitions and offers!

Follow us
@BoldwoodBooks
@BookandTonic

Sign up to our weekly deals newsletter

https://bit.ly/BoldwoodBNewsletter

Printed in Great Britain
by Amazon

43140963R00126